The Rescue

Alana Siegel

Olivia Hart and the Gifted Program: The Rescue

By: Alana Siegel

* * * *

* * * *

To my bridesmaids. As individuals, I admire the countless positive traits that make each of you unique and magnificent people, and thank you for inspiring Jaime's patience and skill, Helen's magnetism and friendship, and Chelsea's altruism and loyalty. It is no coincidence that Olivia is surrounded by wonderful friends, as I am fortunate to be friends with the five of you.

* * * *

Table of Contents

* * * *

Chapter One: Sliced Down the Middle

Justin Benz reached up and touched the tips of his fingers to the window from the inside of his two-door silver Accord. With his usual concentration, his hand was steady, his sea foam eyes were focused, and his thin lips sat in a straight line above his perfectly chiseled jaw line. Despite his stoic features, an immense power oozed from his fingers. The air filled with blue Gifted electricity and tickled my skin.

Ping. Ping. Ping. Tiny pieces of glass, smaller than grains of sand, made popping noises as they chipped off the window beneath his fingers. I watched as larger cracks appeared. They weaved their way across the length of the car, dancing from corner to corner of each glass pane.

A low gurgling sound emerged from the car's leather interior as a black inky substance, melted from Justin's touch, careened its way through the cracks, fused with the glass, and healed the flaws.

Justin let out a controlled breath, content now that the windows were tinted. Placing his left hand on the wheel and his right on the gearshift, he put the car in drive and we sped down the streets of Pandora, hidden from prying eyes.

I took a breath in through my nose, held it for a few seconds, and then unsteadily let the air rush out of my lungs. The movement caught Justin's attention, and he placed his hand on top of mine in an attempt to comfort me. Justin was a little too aware of my uneasiness. I immediately felt guilty, and for the thousandth time this week, reminded myself to take quieter breaths.

I looked over at him sitting in the driver's seat and gave him a forced smile to assure him that I was perfectly fine. I must have convinced him because he returned my display with a crooked grin of his own that stirred the butterflies in my stomach. I knew it wasn't right to pretend to have it all together, but I felt a teensy bit better knowing Justin wasn't worried.

I wanted to revel in the attention Justin could now pay me freely. I was ecstatic that he finally made room for me in his lone-wolf life. Every once in awhile we allowed ourselves to get lost on cloud nine, but the escape proved bittersweet each time we returned to reality.

Justin was protective of me. No, protective didn't cover it. He was *obsessed* with my safety and happiness. He blamed himself for everything bad that ever happened to me. He brooded over the fact that he caused me sadness when he tried to keep our relationship a secret, he kicked himself for not protecting me from Prometheus's obsession, and he beat himself up because I had to follow him to the middle of the Nevada desert to learn that it had been Prometheus who sent my Gifted necklace and Justin's pocketknife to Pandora.

Considering all that had happened in such a short time, I couldn't believe our retreat in Salt Lake City, and search for answers at the Prometheus's Fort Bliss, was only a week ago. It felt far longer ago, and I was frustrated that, instead of answers, we had only found more questions.

One thing I knew for sure: Prometheus hated the Meta. The Meta was the governing body for the Gifted, and Prometheus wasn't alone in his loathing. Feeling pressure from other governments who unfairly blamed tough times on the Gifted, the Meta turned against the people it was created to protect. For decades, the Meta had caused more problems than it solved, and thousands of Gifted were captured, never to be seen again, including Great Aunt Ev's fiancé.

It was in the middle of Fort Bliss that Justin finally explained to me that Prometheus had visited him throughout his childhood, speaking about Gifted glory and his inevitable marriage to me, an act meant to piss off the Meta.

A stranger announcing your future nuptials would be jarring enough for a five-year-old boy, but the bigger fear was the Meta would hear about this intended ceremony. The Meta outlawed the union of Elste girls and Horus boys eons ago when Pyramus and Thisbe's secret love affair caused the Gifted Wars. After hearing of Great Aunt Ev's calamitous run-in at her aborted wedding, the wrath of the Meta would keep anyone up at night.

I hadn't known about Prometheus's meddlesome visits to Pandora. When Justin finally told me everything, I told him I didn't care. There was no governing body, tragic love story, or diabolical force that would keep us apart. I loved him.

I had hoped my word, and my love, would relieve some of the burden he had carried for so long. I still meant every word, but I had no idea what following my heart to Salt Lake City would mean for my friends.

Focusing on the present, I loosened my death grip on the books in my lap. Slowly, I unhooked each finger and stretched them until they were smooth.

Somehow, I was still waking up and heading to class at Pandora High School, in the makeshift and dilapidated old building across town the school board sent us to after the high school building was destroyed last fall. The rest of the town thought a tornado was to blame, but we knew the destruction was caused by immense Gifted powers when we had our first run-in with Prometheus's crew in Ms. Magos's secret room.

Months later, Mr. Rowling still liked to assign lengthy papers, the baseball team still played their games after school, and Mr. Stackhouse still had trouble communicating to his students. From an outsider's view, Pandora was an average suburban town, but as long as the only female Elste in the world lived here, it was anything but average.

Justin pulled into the teacher's lot in the front of the school and parked his car in the first spot. The notion that I was worried about making it to class on time felt surreal. There were so many other pressing things to stress about.

I stepped out of the passenger side, and Justin hurried to meet me. I watched his confident strides. He may still be wearing jeans and a zip-up hoodie, but he looked older, mature, and sure of himself. Or maybe he was rejuvenated with a new purpose in life: taking care of me.

Keeping his eyes level with mine, he pushed my hair behind my ear. The slight touch of his fingers sent his Gift coursing through my body, heating up my veins, and causing my knees to go weak. It felt soothing and comforting, and it reminded me that I needed to pay more attention. It was too easy to step aside and let him block all evil from hurting me. I wouldn't allow him to bear the brunt of my problems.

"Are you okay?" he whispered. After the year we had, he pulled himself together while I was falling apart at the seams. Why did our trip to the Midwest have the opposite effect on me? Nevertheless, I nodded to persuade him I was all right. He kissed my cheek, intertwined our fingers, and turned to lead me to the front door.

As we walked, I scanned the row of windows along the building until I spotted Mr. Dimon. I wasn't surprised to see him but the sight of him caused my blood to boil. He was an agent for the Meta, and he doubled as the school's superintendent in order to keep an eye on us. In his sharp charcoal suit and short haircut, he stood with his arms folded, eying us through his office window.

He was the one who announced Justin's name at the student lottery drawing last week, forcing us to use the parking spot in the teacher's lot. At the time, a bunch of kids had clapped Justin on the back, shouting about how lucky he was. It had taken all my energy not to blast them with the dark side of my Gifted charm. Luck, indeed. The manufactured victory allowed Mr. Dimon to watch us like a hawk.

The shock of the previous week hit me as his surly expression bore into me. The memories were torturous as I relived the moment I regained consciousness in Prometheus's mansion, discovered the Gifted Program had been sliced in half, and realized it was Mr. Dimon who had completed the amputation. Helen O'Reilly, Jaime Forte, Max Smarr, Ms. Magos, Prometheus's Horus named Hunter, and my brother Derek had all been hauled off to the Meta's prison cells.

Without input from anyone else, Prometheus and the school's superintendent decided who went to the Meta and who was sent to Pandora. They chose sides like we were going to play dodge ball in gym class.

Apparently, Prometheus bartered with Mr. Dimon, convincing him that there was one person the Meta wanted to capture more than the female Elste, and that was himself. Personally, I wasn't sure what the Meta would want with a vapid old man like Prometheus.

I didn't even get to say goodbye to my friends before Mr. Dimon took the rest of us back to Pandora. When we asked about them, he threatened their wellbeing unless we followed his rules.

Prometheus was the maestro who had, yet again, dictated my life, but it was easy to hate Mr. Dimon just as much, especially when I had to watch him gloat over his successful capture of my friends.

I grasped my charm necklace and smelled my Gifted rose scent as Justin and I walked past his window. I was no longer the weak, shy girl hiding in the back of the class. I knew that no matter what any bully did, I could do much worse. Every inch of my body filled with power. It would be so easy to target Mr. Dimon and overwhelm him with sadness and gloom. Besides, that's how he made me feel. It would only be fair to share it.

"Hurting him won't get them back, Liv," Justin whispered and squeezed my hand. "He's not worth it."

I shook my head as if to clear it of the evil thoughts. If Thisbe caused an entire Gifted War, I didn't want to find out what my anger would do. I looked down at the mood ring Justin gave me. A bloodlust red swirled through the stone, and prompted me to keep my emotions in check. It was a life saving tool and reminded me of the importance of control.

I sighed. Our friends were locked in the Meta's prison because of me. I was positive that the Meta would have settled for the capture of the only destructive Elste in the world, but thanks to Prometheus and Mr. Dimon, my friends were taken instead.

I could prove my treacherous power right here and now, and everyone would realize the Meta arrested the wrong people, but Justin was right. Hurting Mr. Dimon wouldn't get my friends back. I promised myself the day we were separated that no one would suffer from the burden of being a friend of the only female Elste—not Derek, not Helen, not Justin—no one. The challenge in front of me was to control my emotions and figure out how to keep that promise and get those friends freed.

* * * *

Chapter Two: Bent, Not Broken

As we walked in the front doors, I concentrated on putting one foot in front of the other. The cadence of my steps wasn't in sync with anyone else. It felt really obvious to me, even if no one else noticed. All my senses were heightened. Smells were more potent. Colors were more vivid. I felt different. I was different…but I wasn't alone.

With our hands linked, Justin and I scanned the throngs of students who huddled with friends or rushed to class with their arms full of books. To everyone else, it was just a regular school day. Not for me. Regular wasn't in my vocabulary anymore. I was anxious and on guard and ready for an army of Meta agents to jump out from behind a group of ninth grade girls at any moment.

I looked to my right and saw Luca Hale. He was watching me from his new locker at the end of the hall. His dark skin couldn't hide the purple circles under his eyes, but somehow, broody looked handsome on him.

He gave me half a smile. It wasn't one of his dazzling white toothy grins, but it managed to calm me and loosen some of the knots in my stomach.

With his backpack opened on the floor and books scattered in front of him, he followed Mr. Dimon's demand that we blend with the student body.

That was just one item on the long list of requirements. The list included cutting Luca off from all contact with Aunt Ev in Salt Lake City. I knew the seclusion from the woman who treated him like family drove him crazy, but he refused to act out and risk the lives of our friends in prison. The group sent to Pandora was nothing more than a hodgepodge of former Gifted Program members and soldiers from Prometheus's crew. Tension was high and trust was wearing thin. I didn't know how to tell Luca how grateful I was to have him here.

While Luca's eyes watched me, he nodded at Graham who leaned lazily against the wall next to him and rambled on as if he had Luca's full attention. During the first few days in Pandora, Luca had peppered Mr. Dimon with questions. He asked what the Meta planned to do with us. He questioned Aunt Ev's safety, and he begged to know when he could leave. Each nagging question irked Mr. Dimon and didn't produce any answers. Luca realized his digging wasn't helping. The Meta was going to keep us in the dark.

Luca was an expert at reading people, understanding a situation, and judging a group's mood. However, his best friend, Graham Roberts, was the opposite.

Graham was Prometheus's Ikos, and although Luca fell back into an easy friendship with Graham, I still had a hard time trusting him. After months of fearing Prometheus and his crew, it was hard to reconcile that we were now on the same side, fighting the Meta. Sure, I felt bad that he was forced to live in Pandora, but as far as I could tell, Graham only cared about two things: hooking up with girls and getting into fights.

In a trendy dark tank top, Graham displayed his rippling arm muscles. He whipped his head back to clear his long, dirty blonde surfer hair from his face. From the moment he stepped through Pandora's doors, his overconfidence and physique attracted lots of attention. One look at his cocky grin and you knew that was exactly what he had hoped for.

Justin looped his arm around my waist. I glanced at his face and caught him staring coolly at Luca. Whether it was distrust because Justin hadn't gotten to know Luca like the rest of us at the Gifted retreat or just plain jealousy, Justin was extra protective when Luca was around. I set my hand on his arm to assure him we were safe and led him down the hall.

Promising refuge and security was another white lie I told, and I constantly felt guilty. The truth was everyone who hung around me was in danger. Justin should walk away from this debacle. He wasn't obligated to free our friends or fight the Meta. Prometheus had forced him to fall for me. He was sucked in because I loved him, and I couldn't let him go.

I spent hours thinking about it. Why did Prometheus pick Justin? He could have picked any male Horus. His own loyal guard Hunter was a Horus. On the other hand, as the only female Elste, I had no choice but to keep going with this mission, and I was dragging Justin with me.

I hugged my books and leaned against the cool surface as Justin spun the combination of the slim metal locker we shared. Thinking about anything we shared caused the corners of my lips to tip up. Even if the world was crumbling around us, we were together for real this time. He was my boyfriend, and everyone knew it.

The fleeting surge of happiness faded with incredulity at how quickly things had changed. It was only two weeks ago I had fallen to pieces when Justin thought he could spare me from Prometheus's master plan by breaking up with me. I had flown to Salt Lake City overwhelmed with loneliness.

I clenched my jaw as I remembered the cost of my newfound happiness with Justin. I went to the middle of the desert to get answers and wound up losing my friends. As morose and broken as I had felt then, the emotions paled in comparison to the immense fury and helplessness I felt now. I was full of anger and a lust to fight, but I was being guarded like a caged animal.

I had balled my hands into fists by the time Cliff Adams hurried toward us. With his thick, long hair messier than usual and his eyebrows furrowed, he didn't look like the bubbly pitcher on the baseball team we saw a week ago. These days his shoulders sagged, and the frazzled sight of him reminded me that I needed to appear composed. I pushed away my frustrated nerves.

"Olivia, is the Gifted Program meeting tonight?" he asked without saying hello.

"Hey man, I heard you're starting pitcher at the next game," Justin announced, attempting to put a smile on his best friend's face.

Cliff nodded, brushing off the compliment as if it was unimportant under the circumstances, and turned back for my answer. Anxiety covered his features.

I stood a little taller. "Of course," I said with false confidence. It wasn't the first time someone in the Gifted Program assumed I was in charge since Derek and Jaime were captured, but I wasn't comfortable in the role yet. I wasn't sure I ever would be.

He looked at me expectantly. "Have you heard from anyone?" He was specifically referring to Helen and hope was written across his face. I hadn't realized how deeply he cared for her, until she was taken away from us. I bit my lip and shook my head no.

He looked down at his feet, and I felt the salt water begin to build in the corner of my own eyes. My involuntary display of emotion made me angry. I knew it was a sign of weakness, and not the reaction of a leader.

To make matters worse, Justin saw the tears. "Cliff, let me walk you to class," he said and threw his arm around his friend's shoulder to pull him down the hall and give me a second to pull myself together.

Luca had been hovering a few feet in the opposite direction, and he took the opportunity to catch me alone. "Liv, how are you holding up?" he asked. His dark eyes reflected his deep concern. I felt the sweetness of his Gift charming me to a carefree place. He knew it calmed me so he always turned it on when I was near. I looked at his charm on the chain around his neck, so much like mine and Derek's. We lit up in a purple glow.

Luca still considered me a friend, and it was difficult to put into words what a relief that was. Perhaps he wasn't giving up hope that one day we would be together. Even with Justin's new display of affection, I refused to give up Luca's friendship. It might not sound fair, but in desperate times like these, I needed his easy warmth.

In fact, fairness was something I often debated. Maybe letting Justin go would make things easier. He couldn't protect me from everything. If I lied and told him I didn't love him, he might suffer less in the long run. I would eventually leave to fight the Meta. Justin wouldn't want me to go, I was certain. If we were already broken up, he wouldn't feel responsible, and I could protect him from a future of despair.

Luca would always support my decision to fight. He was the first to show confidence in the strength of my Gift and tell others how powerful I was. He would understand what I needed to do.

Even as Graham swaggered over to us and broke through my trance, I choked on the idea of telling Justin I didn't love him. "Hey, Olivia," Graham said. His giant body of muscle and sex appeal loomed over me.

"Hey, Graham," I said awkwardly, shifting my weight from foot to foot.

"Is the Gifted Program still meeting tonight?" Graham asked. Despite my uncertainty of Graham, his renewed friendship with Luca gave him a free pass to our secret meetings. He held my gaze, waiting for my command.

16

I stood there between two of the most eligible men in Pandora. "Uhh…yes," I confirmed, trying to sound like the authority figure rather than a high school junior who got tongue-tied in front of cute boys.

"Hi, Olivia," a girl's voice rang out from a pack of passing seniors. Nestled in the middle of the group was the familiar face of a blonde who sat next to me in art class last semester. Claire? Susan? I couldn't remember. We weren't exactly friends.

"Oh, hi…," I stammered and raised my hand to wave. It wasn't like she would have noticed if I never responded. She had zoned in on Luca and Graham.

The girl's suggestive eyes caused army green to waft out from under Graham's shirt like puffs of steam. As they passed us, he kept his vision on her backside, revving his Gift of agility and strength until the group was a few feet in front of us. Cupping his Gifted bracelet, he shouted something about meeting up with us later and took off in the pretty girl's direction at a dizzying speed.

Luca took the opposite approach to the added attention and gossip from the girls. He politely declined their advances while never taking his eyes off me.

Finally alone, Luca leaned in close and ground his teeth as he spat out, "I walked past that rat, Mr. Dimon's, office this morning." I could feel his breath on my ear, and I had to fight the delicious tingle down my back.

Instead, I channeled my anger. "Me too," I vented.

"It's been a whole week, and he hasn't told us anything!! I wanted to rip those beady eyes right out of his head!" Luca fumed. I could feel my own hatred building again.

I whispered, but my anger with Mr. Dimon echoed in each word. "I would have shown him real pain if Justin hadn't held me back."

Luca grabbed both my shoulders and turned me towards him. "Just do it, Liv. Why not? Who cares what Justin says? We are stuck in this small town while our friends are held captive!"

I shook my head, and repeated the line I had said multiple times over the last few days, "Justin is right; we need to come up with a plan. The Meta will expect us to use force. It's what they want."

"No, standing on the sidelines is what Justin wants," Luca stated, his voice louder now.

"Since you know me so well, feel free to elaborate on what I want," Justin pressed, approaching us calmly.

Luca held my gaze for a second before turning to Justin. "You're only concerned with keeping Olivia safe," Luca growled.

"And you're not?" Justin asked, raising his eyebrows, shoving his hands in his pockets, and helping Luca to dig himself into a hole.

"Of course I am," Luca said, lowering his voice. "But there are others who need our help, too."

Luca's frustration with Justin always came close to a breaking point, but he never let it go too far. Before listening to Justin's response, he spun on his heels and walked into Mr. Stackhouse's classroom. I gave Justin my best "was-that-really-necessary?" look.

They had been fighting like cats and dogs since we got to Pandora. It was exhausting to be in the middle of it. Justin's unreadable features didn't make him look apologetic. Instead, he took the global studies book out of my hands and handed over my lab book. Then, he grasped my free hand in his own and led me into Mr. Stackhouse's class.

* * * *

Chapter Three: A Charm Unmanageable

Justin and I parted down the aisle in Mr. Stackhouse's science class, and he joined Cliff at a worn wooden lab desk on the right side of the room while I moved further to the back. The knots in my stomach pulled tight. I hated being alone.

I stared at the empty seat at my station and took a deep breath. I missed Jaime. I wished she were here to tell me what to do or where to start researching.

Releasing the breath, I cleared my head and focused my attention on moving forward. It was my turn to lead. I couldn't disappear into the ground. I needed to be present and functioning. I sat up taller in my seat.

No big deal; I would start small. If I could muster the energy for everyday life, I could move on to bigger things like rescuing my friends from the Meta.

I took out my floppy lab book and opened it. *See, I am independent and able to take care of myself.* I felt a little better.

I dug into my bag for a pencil. I found a sharp pink one, and settled in for a long period of note-taking. Maybe for once Mr. Stackhouse's meandering lesson would distract me from my personal drama rather than bore me.

Snap. My pencil tip cracked off. I glanced at the pencil sharpener that had been broken since January. I sighed. I was already breaking my vow of independence. I would have to ask one of the boys if I could borrow something to write with.

I hadn't even opened my mouth to speak when Luca and Justin both looked back to check on me. It was as if they had microphones surrounding my desk, monitoring my every breath and sigh. I lifted my broken pencil to show them the tip. "Can I borrow...?"

I didn't get to finish my question. They jumped to their feet and scoured their pockets. Luca located a writing utensil first. With a black mechanical pencil in his open hand, he walked toward me. I reached out to take it, but Justin got to Luca's hand first.

He pressed two fingers to the plastic, and the pencil went limp. Its amorphous shape sagged between Luca's fingers and dripped an indistinguishable black material onto the floor.

Luca looked at Justin with a stunned face. "You melted my pencil!"

Justin's blue hue didn't hide his crooked smile. He shrugged his shoulders. "Sorry, but Olivia doesn't like mechanical pencils," he said, transferred his Gifted pocketknife to his free hand, and passed me a classic yellow wooden pencil.

It happened so fast that I didn't have time to scold them for their petty fight. I just took the pencil. Luca clenched his jaw, and the smug look never left Justin's face.

"Everybody, take your seats," Mr. Stackhouse said. "Today, we will be dissecting earthworms." There were an equal number of groans and cheers. My skin turned cold and clammy.

"Mr. Stackhouse, Cliff won't mind doing this experiment by himself. I'll be Olivia's partner for today," Justin announced. Frazzled by Justin's rare, outspoken decision, Mr. Stackhouse nodded and continued setting up.

Luca rose to his feet, immediately. "I'll join them, too. My lab partner can work with Cliff," he added. Mr. Stackhouse began to look suspicious. He tilted his head and narrowed his eyes.

"Not so fast, Luca. I'm sure Justin and Olivia can handle the lesson just fine," he said and motioned with his hand for Luca to sit down. He turned to the board to show the matter was closed.

Luca remained standing. I watched the air around him swirl into a purple cloud. With a twinkle in his eye and his charm dangling around his neck, he leaned one hip against his lab desk, crossed one ankle over the other, and tucked both broad arms around his chest.

"Are you sure about that, Mr. Stackhouse?" Luca challenged. Mr. Stackhouse's body tensed. He was a shy, dorky man, but he was still the authority figure. Twenty pairs of eyes turned to the new kid who dared to disagree with the teacher.

They didn't see what I saw. Luca was lit with Gifted power. It exuded from every inch of his body and seeped around the room like rolling fog.

"Groups of two and three make more sense than forcing anyone to work by themselves, don't you think?" Luca asked, confidently.

Mr. Stackhouse stood there blinking a few times, confused by the need to agree with Luca. "I...uh...guess that makes sense," he stammered. He pushed his glasses up the bridge of his nose.

Luca didn't waste any time and pushed his stool up to my lab station. Justin seethed from my other side. I wanted to lay my head on the desk.

Fed by Luca and Justin's jealous competition, a purple and blue air mass hovered around my desk. It was so powerful and concentrated that it gave me goose bumps.

"Please fill in your worksheets, describing the color, texture, and smell of the earthworm's internal organs," Mr. Stackhouse explained, returning to his lesson. Justin and Luca's evil glares and smug faces were distracting. I tried to focus on the front of the room.

Mr. Stackhouse picked up a jar and popped off the top. "I recommend taking two or three earthworms. They are slippery, and you will most likely destroy a few organs as you investigate others." My stomach churned.

He used a pair of tongs to grab a couple worms and placed them into his petri dish. Then, he passed the jar of worms to the closest pair of students. The girl looked pale and tentative, but the guy dug into the jar with excitement.

I watched it pass between stations until, finally, it arrived at our desk. Justin grabbed the container. He took his time selecting the worms for our experiment, holding the jar tightly.

"Here you go, Luca. You can choose your own," Justin said. The air around him was tinted blue. Something about his sudden shift to nice guy wasn't genuine. With two hands on the jar, he slowly stretched his arms. Luca cocked his head, suspiciously.

"Katherine, would you mind passing the jar of worms?" Luca asked the girl at the desk in front of us. His voice was soothing and sexy.

"Sure thing, Luca." Katherine shot out of her seat and grabbed the container before Justin could object. She had barely taken a step when the glass shattered into hundreds of pieces. Slimy, gooey, brown earthworms covered her hands, clothes, and feet. The pressure from the exploding jar was so great that there were even earthworms in her hair.

"Katherine, are you okay? What bad luck," Luca exclaimed with genuine concern for Katherine as an innocent bystander as well as delight in thwarting Justin's set-up. He struggled to appear sympathetic while smiling arrogantly because he had won the round. Justin looked horrified and helpless as Katherine slid through the mounds of worms on the floor to the sink. Justin had obviously caused the build-up of pressure and faint cracks in the glass.

"Alright, everyone. I'll get a janitor in here to clean this up. Luckily, we have enough worms for the experiment. Let's continue," Mr. Stackhouse instructed, attempting to quiet the class and get us back on track.

"Excuse me, Mr. Stackhouse!" Luca shouted over the commotion in the classroom to get the teacher's attention. Again, his Gift was turned on high. The spark of it tingled on my skin. Mr. Stackhouse looked like a dopey puppy as Luca took control of his actions.

"Justin would like to stand in the front of the class and show everyone how to do the experiment," Luca declared. A puff of blue air burst out from Justin. He growled as he launched towards Luca. His open hands reached for his throat.

"ENOUGH!" I shouted. I stood up and felt power building at my center and pulsing out of my hands. Every pair of eyes in the room focused on me, and even Justin and Luca were affected.

My Gift was the strongest. It demanded everyone's attention, but it was involuntary on my part. Our friends were being held as prisoners while Luca and Justin were having a silly jealousy fight. They were foolish, immature, and out of control. My body reacted because I was frustrated and angry.

I bared my teeth. If I adjusted the frequency of my Gift ever so slightly, then Justin and Luca would feel my anger. I watched as the classroom cringed in pain.

No, that was wrong. I glanced at the ring on my finger. It was a gory red. I was too powerful and dangerous. I bit my lip and tried to focus on what was really important. Quickly, I changed my own emotions, picturing a clear night sky, feeling a brotherly hug from Derek, smelling my mom's lasagna. The mood of the entire class switched as I concentrated on happier things. It all happened in a matter of seconds.

I dried my sweaty palms on my pants, and spoke in a calm voice, "I'm ready to continue the lesson." Then, I sat back down, releasing everyone from my trance.

* * * *

Chapter Four: Teacher's Pet

I was wrong. There were things I hated far more than being alone. I hated being in the middle of a petty fight. I hated not knowing how to save my friends. And I hated the fact that I was dangerous, and I mean accidentally-torture-my-boyfriend dangerous. Justin and Luca recovered quickly enough from my blast of sadness, but it didn't change the fact that I did it. I felt guilty.

At the end of Mr. Stackhouse's earthworm dissection, I rattled off excuses why I needed a minute alone, and wedged myself free from Justin and Luca. If the lab session taught me anything, it was how dangerously fast my anger could be sparked, and this made one thing clear: I had to fight the Meta alone. It was the safest way.

I couldn't risk the lives of the ones I loved, and if they were standing in the line of fire, I wasn't sure I would be able to turn off my Gift next time. The Gifted Program would not take the news well that I intended to fight alone, so I would wait and tell them when the time was right. Maybe I was a coward for putting off the uncomfortable conversation, but for now, we would search for our friends together.

I was still riled up when I arrived at Mr. Rowling's English class a minute early and stopped in the hallway outside his door just as Lynn Vapor sauntered into the room and took a seat in the back. An air of detachment and superiority surrounded her, and it wasn't just because she could use her Gift to fade into the background, or turn up when you least expected her.

Knowing her piercing blue eyes were watching me from on top of her high horse didn't help my mood. She was Prometheus's Hadean, and my brother's ex-girlfriend. He had thought they were in love, but as far as I could tell, she had only dated him to spy on us at school. Lynn had lied and manipulated far worse than anyone else in Prometheus's crew, and I wasn't sure I would ever trust her.

Since we arrived in Pandora, she kept her distance. She played the role as Mr. Dimon had asked her, showing up to class each day and pretending to be a Pandora student, but she didn't speak to any of us. I wondered what was going on inside that sly blonde head of hers.

I wished I could call Derek. I missed his lighthearted banter and brotherly advice. I was supposed to be filling in his shoes, but I was doing a poor job of it. How was I supposed to keep the Gifted Program focused on rescuing our friends?

I was still standing in the doorway of Mr. Rowling's classroom, deep in thought, when Chelsea Steinem, all four foot eleven of her, ran up to me.

Her long blonde hair was pushed back in her silver Gifted headband, and it swished behind her. Despite her height, she was a fierce fighter. She grabbed my shoulder, jolting me out of my thoughts. She took two deep breaths before she could speak. "I...heard...Mrs. Wolf...on the phone again," she panted.

I could smell her vanilla Gifted scent, and I gave her a look of disapproval. "Chelsea, I thought you weren't going to do that anymore. It's too dangerous," I scolded.

Chelsea shook her head violently. "Liv, you don't understand. There are millions of Gifted in the world who are being oppressed by the Meta," she exclaimed.

After learning about the Gifted community in Salt Lake City, Chelsea took on the troubles of all the Gifted in the world and spent half of her time invisibly listening in to conversations in hopes of hearing about Gifted outside Pandora. I sighed because her heartfelt care to fight for what was right was impressive, but completely unsafe.

"Would it help us if Mrs. Wolf catches you listening and hands you over to the Meta?" I asked.

About a week ago, we figured out that Mrs. Wolf was Gifted, a descendant of the Ikos family, and Mr. Dimon knew it. We never confronted her, but we were pretty sure they had some unspoken agreement allowing Mrs. Wolf to stay in Pandora as the school nurse.

"It wouldn't help, but that doesn't matter. I never get caught," Chelsea replied, looking smug. I clicked my tongue. I was frustrated with her insistence on pushing Mr. Dimon's buttons. I loved Chelsea, but I missed my easy friendship with Helen. I reminded myself that Chelsea wasn't supposed to be filling in for her. I would find Helen.

"You're missing the point," she said, exasperated that I wasn't following her logic. "Mrs. Wolf has a sister." My own frustration already building, I looked at her with slim interest.

"A Gifted sister who lives near the Meta," she added. My jaw dropped as the realization set in. She could tell us where our friends were being held captive.

"Where is the Meta?" I asked her with growing interest. The bell to begin the period rang. Students were taking their seats and opening their books.

"I don't know yet, but I'm going to find out," Chelsea said. She was smiling, happy to have convinced me that she was doing the right thing.

Mr. Rowling put his hands on hips in the front of the classroom. "Chelsea and Olivia, six months ago I couldn't keep you in the same room without you ripping each other's hair out. You can extend your newfound friendship in detention today after school," he said and turned dismissively to write on the board.

I stared at his back with disbelief. Detention was the last thing I needed. Chelsea turned to me with her eyes wide, trying to send a message without speaking out loud.

I shook my head once. I knew she wanted me to use my Gift to convince Mr. Rowling not to give us detention.

"Jaime wouldn't approve," I argued.

"And look where that got her," Chelsea countered, harshly.

Now it was Mr. Rowling's turn to stare in disbelief. "Girls, find your seats or you'll start your detention right now," he scolded. Chelsea stamped her heel down on my big toe.

"Oww...we...ahhh...," I stuttered between clenched teeth. Mr. Rowling crossed his arms and waited for my excuse. My Gift ignited and a burst of rose perfume exuded from me. I concentrated on happy thoughts. I pictured Justin reaching for my hand in a crowd, Helen dancing on the football field at kickline practice, and Derek laughing wildly at some joke. I hoped my Gift was the happy version and not the doom and gloom it had been lately. "We were just...," I stumbled again, but now Chelsea could smell my Gift and knew Mr. Rowling would do whatever we said.

The victim of my charm, Mr. Rowling's eyebrows slowly rose from their narrowed position on his head. His whole face lightened.

"We were just wondering if you could mix in some books on the reading list with strong, female characters. Catherine Earnshaw and Elizabeth Bennett are hardly characters to look up to," Chelsea argued, saving me from my inability to speak.

Mr. Rowling's jaw hung open. His head bobbled up and down in assent. As Chelsea spoke to him, his eyes never left my face. I looked at him from under my long lashes and held his gaze. The power and control felt wonderful, but it still didn't feel like the right thing to do.

"Great, and since that was all we were trying to say, we no longer need to go to detention, right?"

He nodded his head again with the exuberance of a little boy who's been told he will get ice cream for being good. Chelsea elbowed me to sit down. I released Mr. Rowling and walked to my seat.

Someone in the back row pretended to cough into his hand and shouted, "Teacher's pet!"

* * * *

Chapter Five: Play Ball

Side by side, Justin and I leaned against the rusty foul line fence at the Pandora baseball game. The unkempt field was little more than dirt with four bases positioned in a diamond. Every twenty feet or so, sparse blades of grass stood in the wrong places.

The ragged wooden stands were packed with loud spectators watching a game that was already in motion. The scoreboard showed Pandora was tied with Sparta, five to five, in the fourth inning.

"Oh no," Justin groaned, peering out into the field.

"What?" I asked, nervously. Following his gaze, I stared out at the guys on the field, searching for Meta agents.

"Cliff is panicking." Justin sounded worried for his friend. I relaxed and tried not to show my relief that he was only concerned for his friend's well-being and not an attack from terrifying and buff agents.

From where we stood, I couldn't make out which players were on the field, but I focused my attention at the center, knowing Cliff was standing on the pitcher's mound. He attempted to wipe the sweat off his forehead with the back of his hand, but new drops appeared too quickly. He angrily spit on the ground next to him, dug his left toe into the dirt, and cradled the ball in his mitt at chest level.

The batter was a small wiry kid. With his knees bent and the bat in ready position, he was prepared to swing. Cliff wound up and awkwardly lobbed the ball. Out of the corner of my eye, I saw Justin cringe.

"Adams!" The coach scolded from the dugout. The catcher had to jump up and reach out to catch the ball. Cliff punched the air and kicked the dirt.

The catcher tossed the ball back to Cliff. He went through the same preparations as the last pitch, trying to calm his nerves.

"Come on, Cliff," Justin muttered in encouragement.

The ball was thrown with slightly better accuracy. *CRACK*. The bat connected with the ball and sent it soaring into left field. The Sparta fans cheered wildly, their eyes following the ball through the air.

My attention was drawn in a different direction, and my eyes didn't immediately follow the ball. My body tensed up as I focused on the army green mushroom cloud that appeared in right field. Since when was someone Gifted on the school's baseball team?

I squinted my eyes as a virile blur ran faster and jumped higher than humanly possible. He slowed down only in order to reach over the player in the left outfield position and catch the ball effortlessly. As he landed back on the ground with so much natural grace that it looked like he was posing for pictures, I recognized Graham Robert's confident grin. I felt an unexpected adrenaline rush of pleasure as the umpire called the batter out.

"That's right, suckers!" Graham taunted the Spartan dugout before completing a victory dance.

"Wow, impressive catch. I didn't know Graham was playing baseball for Pandora," I said, feeling guilty that Graham had used his Gift to help the team…but it was, after all, my high school team. I turned to Justin. He wasn't wearing the same broad smile as the Pandora fans. In fact, he was scowling at Graham.

"What's he playing at?" Justin growled. I wiped the smile off my face and silently watched the teams switch positions. I wasn't sure if he was mad at Graham for using his Gift so obviously in front of spectators, or for showing off and cleaning up Cliff's mess, or just because he didn't trust him. I remained silent as I watched Graham hop to the dugout and Cliff drag his feet.

The Sparta pitcher was built like a gorilla. His biceps flexed as he sneered in the batter's direction. He threw the first pitch hard and straight into the catcher's mitt. Sparta's fans cheered. The second and third pitches were just as quick and flawless, and the second batter faced more of the same.

Come on, Pandora, I cheered in my head. I was bit by the competitive bug, and I didn't want my team to lose. The next Pandora batter, wearing lucky number seven, didn't look as worried as I felt. I squinted, but couldn't make out his face hidden in his helmet. He took his time approaching home base, hitting the bottom of his cleats with the end of his bat before stepping up to the plate.

By the time the pitcher wound up to complete the throw, I knew exactly who was batting. Luca looked like a glowing purple mirage. Fans called out his name. They must have seen him up at bat before. He wiggled on the mound, pretending to adjust his stance, but I was sure he just wanted a rise out of the crowd. I started to wonder if the five other runs were his.

The ogre who stood on the pitcher's mound let out a girly giggle. His mood was clearly affected by Lucas's Gift, and his throw wasn't much more manly. It made Luca look like a professional baseball player joking around in the minor leagues as he took his time swinging and smashing the ball into the outfield. It was a home run, and Luca ran like a winning champion around the bases. Justin let out a sound of disgust. I tried not to cheer too hard.

The crowd didn't lose its fervor, even though the next batter didn't have Luca's skill, and the pitcher seemed to have regained his masculinity. Three fast outs later, Pandora was picking up their mitts for the field.

"Adams!" Halfway to the mound, Cliff turned around to the coach. "You're out for the rest of the game. Roberts's taking over."

Cliff's anger was palpable as he stamped off the field. Justin hurried after him.

* * * *

Chapter Six: Who's Your Leader?

"So, what's the plan?" Graham pressed. He was leaning forward on a rusted metal chair with his elbows braced on his knees in the basement of the school. He showed little restraint in general, but he didn't hold back his Gifted qualities at all when he was in the presence of only Gifted: his foot tapped against the floor at an unbelievable speed causing tufts of army green swirls to billow from under his shoes.

I took an uneven breath from my claustrophobic position. I was sandwiched between Justin and Chelsea on the ragged and dusty couch. With Cliff sulking in the far right corner avoiding Graham's line of vision, and Luca stuffed in the other, trying not to watch me and Justin, we were definitely over the limit of people that could comfortably fit in the room. I blinked a few times, still not used to the fact that they all looked to me for answers. "Umm...I'm not sure..."

"I think we should storm the Meta," Graham concluded without skipping a beat, as if we were in a war room instead of the prop closet.

"And where do you suggest we go storming, genius? We don't know where the Meta is," Chelsea pointed out. She shot off the couch and began pacing in the small amount of space that didn't contain a glittery sign, costume petticoats, or a human body. The scent of vanilla was left in her wake. She shook out her left hand, which had a habit of disappearing when she was frustrated.

"Calm down, Chelsea. Don't blame Graham," Luca defended. Everyone's Gift was stuck on high; even the air around Luca was slightly purple.

"He's impulsive, like Max and Ms. Magos, and see what happened to them," Chelsea complained.

"Okay, Graham wants to take action, but Max and Ms. Magos are different. They were deceitful," Luca explained.

"That's one thing we can agree on. Max is worthless," Justin chimed in through gritted teeth. With his arm slung over the couch behind me, he sat very still. If you didn't know where to look, he appeared calm, but I saw his hands clenched into fists, his jaw stiff, and of course, he couldn't hide the blue cloud that appeared when he spoke about Max.

"Personally, I don't care if we leave Max at the Meta to rot in prison," Chelsea shouted. She threw her hands in the air like it was easily decided. Justin and Luca nodded their heads in agreement.

I jumped to my feet, shocked at the ability of the group to make our friend the scapegoat. "Max should not be the target of our anger. He's an important member of this Gifted Program!"

I looked around the crowded room. Choosing the basement for our Gifted Program had been a thoughtful and premeditated decision. The long, steep staircase, dark halls, creaky door, and collection of mismatched props conjured up emotions every time I stepped inside. It was once my escape from the prying eyes of gossipy students, and then a refuge to feel the magic between Justin and me. Then it was a place of anger and sadness when Justin lied and said he didn't love me.

The energy and emotion that I felt inside the four walls fueled me with power, and was why I suggested we use it as a safe haven.

"We need to remember who is on our side. Mr. Dimon is the enemy, not Max and his sister," I announced. Everyone's eyes were focused on me, and for once, that made me feel stronger, not uncomfortable.

"Why does Mr. Dimon get to shoulder all the blame?" Lynn's voice cut through the tense room. I glared at the empty space it came from. Her body slowly came into focus, beginning with her head, and then her loud red shirt, and finally her hands and feet. The smell of apples wafted past her, overpowering all other smells in the room.

Since she had kept her distance from all of us since we arrived in Pandora, I hadn't exactly invited her to the meeting. I should have figured she would have overheard and come anyway.

"Shouldn't Prometheus get his fair piece of the bad-guy pie?" she pushed.

"Prometheus isn't bad. He taught us to take pride in being Gifted and not cower at a Meta agent's puny orders," Graham argued. The army color at his feet began to swirl faster.

"But did he tell you that he was going to send you to die of normal-life boredom in a small town?" Lynn's hands were planted on her hips as she glared down at Graham. I shivered because the whole room smelled suddenly like a chilly autumn night.

"He had no choice. The Meta was going to take all of us to prison!" The rest of the room sat still as the two of them volleyed arguments back and forth.

"Prometheus is who created each of you. He was the mastermind behind every delivery of Gifted jewelry in Pandora, every attack on your friends, and every single heartbreak," she said with annoying confidence and surety. She flickered from view, emphasizing each word with the intensity of her Gift.

"Is that true? That's impossible," I said.

"There's a reason he's in control, and it's not because he has any Gift," she replied, slinking onto the couch in my spot.

"Prometheus doesn't have a Gift?!?" Chelsea's voice ended in a shriek in her shock and astonishment.

"Only if you count being cunning as a Gift," Lynn told her.

"How did he get so powerful?" I asked.

"Prometheus was the Meta employee who discovered a way to control the Gifted: mulberry juice is the one thing that turns off a Gift," she said, looking me in the eye. My frustration with Lynn's takeover of my meeting disappeared and was replaced with fear. It was entirely possible that Prometheus spent years orchestrating the mess we were in.

"Prometheus knew the Meta would use it against the Gifted. To this day, the mulberry elixir is a heavily guarded secret, allowing the Meta to prove its prowess and gain approval from the other governments who fear the Gifted. Prometheus believes sharing the secret of the mulberry elixir with the Gifted gives us a chance to defend ourselves, just like the immortal Titan god Prometheus giving fire to humans, and so he claims the name," Lynn explained. Her face twisted in a disgusted sneer.

I went numb as a memory washed over me of the red liquid Prometheus sprayed when we were at Fort Bliss. The moment it hit everyone Gifted, they lost their powers. "He doesn't need a Gift when he has complete power over everyone who is Gifted," I whispered, awestruck by the sudden realization.

"Almost everyone," Luca reminded me. "The mulberry elixir doesn't work on a female Elste."

"Why would he give Olivia an Elste necklace if she would be able to rebel against him?" Cliff spoke up for the first time.

"I have no clue," Lynn snapped. "It's almost as strange as the fact that he told us he was rebelling against the very same government he used to create weapons for." Lynn looked at her manicure as if the important details were nothing more than an afterthought.

Graham jumped out of his seat and his green storm cloud followed. The metal legs of the chair screeched against the floor. "That's not fair, Lynn! Don't change the details of the story so you can blame someone else for the things that you did," he yelled. "Prometheus wasn't a killer, he was a chemist for the Meta, and they exiled him. He hates the Meta just as much as we do."

Graham leaned forward with his hands raised, ready to pounce on Lynn. She vanished from thin air before he grabbed her. Graham stood breathing heavily in the middle of the tiny room.

"You fight like a girl!" he shouted while looking around. A collection of hats and a box of costume jewelry flew across the room and smashed into the back of his head. For a split second, Graham was only a blur across the room. When he reappeared, so did Lynn. He held her arms behind her back.

"Say you give in," he barked in her ear. She struggled against his hold, but it was no use.

"Fine! I give in," she yelled back. Graham gave an evil grin.

"Say Prometheus is always right," he commanded. Instead, she elbowed him in the stomach. He grunted and released his grip. Lynn went back to her seat on the couch.

We were silent as they glared at each other from across the room. I took a long look at each face around the room, and it dawned on me: Only Chelsea and Cliff were as surprised as I was to find out Prometheus used to work for the Meta. Everyone else had known. Justin's jaw was unclenched; a sign the news wasn't jarring. Luca was well prepared to comfort me because he knew I would be thrown by the fact that Prometheus created a female Elste. And Graham and Lynn shared an entire past with the man.

"No one thought it would be wise to share this information with me a week ago?" I asked. The room remained silent as everyone found somewhere to look other than my face. I sighed. "Meeting dismissed."

* * * *

Chapter Seven: One Direction

The building currently housing Pandora High School may have dark and dingy halls, but they were filled with vibrant distractions. I fought to concentrate as a sophomore boy with a backward baseball hat chased after his friend, begging to copy his homework. I sidestepped to avoid having my feet trampled, and instead I knocked into four giggling freshman girls watching a senior flex before grabbing a book from his locker. When I finally managed to get around the group, I almost got sucked into a teacher's lecture on the effects of global warming.

Turning the corner, I huffed out a breath. It wouldn't matter if my favorite male celebrity ran by naked. Nothing was going to stop me from achieving my goal. I was headed in one direction: to Mr. Dimon's office.

I stayed awake all night, analyzing Lynn's story about Prometheus. In the morning, I got up feeling unrested and full of questions.

Why was Prometheus exiled from the Meta? Does he really want to empower the Gifted with the knowledge of the mulberry elixir? And what was the point of creating a destructive female Elste?

All the hours missing sleep in an attempt to arrive at answers about Prometheus were wasted. By the time I got to school, I decided I didn't care about Prometheus. The only way to save my friends was to go directly to Mr. Dimon and get some answers.

What was the worst he could do? Tell me to go away? Does he have the guards at the Meta on speed dial and every time I ask a question, Helen gets tortured?

I bit my bottom lip, feeling unsure. It sounded silly and unreasonable, but they were slyer than we thought. They found us in the middle of the Nevada desert!

I stopped walking. Maybe this was a mistake. Maybe I shouldn't threaten Mr. Dimon.

But wait, Mr. Dimon was merely a pawn in Prometheus's game. The Meta only found us because Prometheus wanted them to. He put the idea of love in Justin's head, and when the superintendent caught on that there was a spark between a Horus boy and an Elste girl, he followed us. Mr. Dimon wasn't as scary or as well-thought out as Prometheus; He was just good at taking hints and following orders.

I nodded my head and kept walking. Mr. Dimon's office was at the end of the next hallway. All I needed to do was make a right and continue straight. I picked up my speed, power walking around a pimpley freshman, a couple kissing in front of their lockers, and a few lacrosse players tossing a ball between them.

I was practically jogging as I rounded the corner, which was why I let out a grunt as I crashed into a tall torso and spindly limbs.

"Olivia, I'm so sorry! I didn't see you coming around the corner," Mary, a friend of Jaime's from the basketball team, apologized and reached out a hand to balance me.

"No, it was my fault. Don't worry about it," I said. I was hoping to continue down the hall again, but she wasn't ready to let go of my arm. "Is everything okay?" I asked.

Mary's eyebrows formed a concerned upside-down V on the top of her head. "I'm actually glad we ran into each other. I'm worried about Jaime. She hasn't returned any of my texts or calls," she said.

"I'm sure she's just busy," I replied, waving my hand like it was no big deal. Mary didn't look convinced, and she wasn't going to let me off easy.

"I stopped by Jaime's house yesterday and her mom said she was selected for a special honors trip," she explained, hinting she knew there was more to the story. I was at a loss for words. I had wondered what lies Mr. Dimon fed to our friend's families. We were banned from visiting them, of course. I could feel the fiery anger growing inside.

I straightened my back, ready to let out a string of angry names for Mr. Dimon when someone let out a yip of fright. I shifted my weight and peered around Mary.

I saw Mrs. Wolf backing into her nurse's office in an odd sort of way. Her mouth was set in an O-shape like she was preparing to scream, and her hands were raised and open by her sides like she was trying not to make any sudden movements. That would have been strange enough, but her eyes were wide with terror and focused on me.

Mary glanced over her shoulder to see what I was staring at. Fear crossed her face as she looked at Mrs. Wolf. "Olivia, what's going on?" she blurted out, looking back at me.

I pasted as genuine a smile as I could manage on my face. "Nothing; I'm sure Jaime's just very busy. They still give you homework on school trips, you know," I said, trying to comfort Mary, but I knew my voice sounded hollow. I took her by the elbow and led her away from Mrs. Wolf's office.

"Okay, you must be right," Mary said, not exactly convinced, but I think my insistence was making her uncomfortable. "If you speak to her, tell her to give me a call." She walked down the hall like she couldn't wait to get away from me. I felt guilty that I hadn't assuaged her concerns.

I turned back toward Mr. Dimon's office with less enthusiasm than before. I snuck a peek in Mrs. Wolf's Pepto-Bismol-pink office but she was gone. Was she scared of something? Was she scared of...me?

My snail's pace was less determined as I walked forward. Sure, I was angry with Mrs. Wolf for cooperating with the Meta, but I'm sure she had a good reason. And yes, I had the power to cause great pain, but I would never hurt her.

"Liv!" Luca's sneakers screeched as he came to a halt in front of me and all worries that Mrs. Wolf was scared of me disappeared from my head. "I'm so glad I caught you!"

I was still upset with Luca because he hadn't shared important information about Prometheus that might help find our friends. I wasn't as angry with Luca as I was with Mr. Dimon, but I still felt my anger reignite and my rose scent blossom. I wouldn't be surprised if everyone in the hallway fainted with exhaustion by the way I whipsawed their emotions with my Gift.

I turned my steely glare on Luca. He grunted as he felt the stab of my anger. I stood my ground, teaching him a lesson.

Luca took a step back and leaned his hands on his knees. "Olivia, I'm sorry I didn't tell you that Prometheus isn't Gifted and that he used to work for the Meta. I only found out from Graham a week ago," he said through the pain.

"You didn't think it would be information I should know?" I asked. The anger was wearing off. My voice was full of disappointment. I was already letting up on my Gift. "Luca, I didn't think we kept secrets from each other," I said in an even softer voice.

Looking into my eyes, he stood up straight and took a step closer to me. "I don't like keeping secrets from you, which is why I have something else to tell you," he said, but the bell rang and we had to sprint to class.

* * * *

Chapter Eight: Mom Knows Best

"Why does Derek want you to bring mulberry tarts next time you visit him?" Mom asked while stirring shrimp scampi with a wooden spoon. I shrugged my shoulders, but kept my eyes glued to the email from Derek.

Mom knew her children better than the back of her own hand. Mulberries were on Derek's list of least favorite foods. I was the only one of my Gifted friends who could stand them. I thought they were delicious. It was an odd trait that went hand in hand with the fact that I was a female Elste and immune to the berry's ability to render the Gifted powerless. I thought Derek's insistence on bringing mulberry tarts was code for 'stick it to the Meta.'

His email had been lighthearted and vague. I thought it was obvious that someone had forced him to write it to keep up the guise that he was busy at school, and his lack of visits shouldn't concern Mom and Dad. I couldn't believe the Meta would stoop so low.

"I don't like the tone of the email," Mom said, reaching for the cordless phone in the corner of our kitchen. Nice try, Meta. You can't fool a mother's instinct. "I'll give him a quick call to check in. He should be in his dorm studying now, anyway."

Panic struck. I rushed over and placed my hand on top of hers. "Mom, I don't think that's such a good idea."

Her eyebrows scrunched together suspiciously. "Olivia, what's going on?" Our hands were still clasped on the phone.

I gave her my best it's-no-big-deal look and let go of the phone. I turned away because I could feel beads of sweat forming on my forehead. It dawned on me that having Derek send an email was smarter than I gave the Meta credit for. They wanted me to break Mr. Dimon's rules. 'Stay quiet or your friends get hurt' was harder when they were testing me. It was a good thing I never made it to Mr. Dimon's office today.

Dad entered the kitchen at that moment. He pushed our ragamuffin cats, Swisher and Carmelo, out of his way. They let out a meow in protest. Dad was too busy opening and closing drawers to notice the awkward moment between Mom and me, and I was grateful.

Mom's laser-like stare lasted a few seconds longer, and then I watched her place the phone back on the counter. At that moment, she must have decided getting to the bottom of my drama was more pressing than worrying about her other child. I was certain she would be able to see right through my lies. I attempted to keep my facial features as smooth as possible.

Her frustration with Dad's endless search for something in the kitchen won over her attention. "What are you looking for!?" she asked with more force than usual. I wiped my sweaty palms on my jeans before she could turn her attention back to me.

"I can't find the notebook Derek uses to track the score of our fantasy team," Dad told her, without stopping his search.

"You can call him after dinner and ask him where he put it," she instructed him.

"No!" I shouted. Both of them looked at me with shocked faces. "I was going to send him an email later. I can ask," I said, without looking at their eyes. A few days without Derek checking in wouldn't worry them too much. He was a freshman, enjoying college life. However, if Derek didn't return an inquiring phone call, their level of worry would definitely increase. I needed to delay them.

I could feel Mom's eyes on me again, but I started shoveling shrimp on my plate instead of letting her read my face. Dad finally noticed the tension in the room and followed my lead, gathering food on his plate instead of igniting the fire by asking questions.

By the time the three of us had settled at the table, Mom seemed more relaxed. I breathed a sigh of relief and lifted a forkful of seafood to my mouth.

"How are things with Helen and Jaime? You haven't said much about them since your trip to Utah," Mom inquired. It sounded like she was hoping to change the subject to something I would feel more comfortable talking about. If she only knew what she was really asking!

I almost spit out the half-chewed food in my mouth. "They're good," I responded, vying for time. Mom wouldn't be okay with such a short answer.

I shoved spaghetti in my mouth, pretending it was too full to speak. She looked at me, expectantly.

"They are on a school trip for honors students," I lied, using Mr. Dimon's fable. My insides were cringing. I was lying to my mom and keeping the Meta's ugly secrets.

She was silent as I pretended to be focused on scraping my fork along the bottom of my plate. When I couldn't stand it any longer, I glanced up at her. She took that as her cue to push on.

"Is this about Max? Is he bullying you again? I can go down to the school and speak to someone about it," she said. Concern and worry dripped from every word.

"No, Mom. Max went on the same trip as Helen and Jaime," I explained, trying to hide my frustration. I wanted to tell her everything. I wanted to ask her advice and remove some of the burden I was carrying. Plus, she deserved to hear the truth. Her only son was locked up somewhere.

"Max is in honors classes?" she asked, her eyebrows twisted high on her forehead.

"Errr...yes," I said, and knew it was too late to explain everything to her. We were in too much trouble; years of plotting and scheming had gone into this plan.

She placed her hand on top of mine. She knew I was lying. I battled with the longing to tell her, but I stopped myself. It was more than the fact that she wouldn't understand. She was defenseless and vulnerable without a Gift, and I would be turning her into a target.

"Olivia," she asked in a softer voice, "is this about Justin? I noticed he drives you to school now."

I actually tasted blood as I bit off my hurtful response to my mom. I was angry with her, but not because she was prying, or because she believed my problems were merely teenage melodrama. I was angry because she didn't recognize that I was stronger than I was before. Powerful enough to cause destruction greater than Max or Justin could even imagine. I was not her broken little girl anymore. I was the female Elste.

* * * *

Chapter Nine: Horus

A giggled escaped from my lips when Justin and I tiptoed past the school gym holding hands. It was drowned out by the sound of a dozen basketballs being dribbled up and down the shiny wood floors. Only seconds later, the teacher blew his whistle and the drilling students stopped bouncing their balls. The thrill of the silence trickled down my spine.

"Shhh," Justin hushed me, but he was smiling when he looked back.

I did a little skip to catch up to him. "I've never cut class before," I whispered with my lips close to his ear.

He turned and wrapped his arms around my waist. "Don't worry. You're not missing much. They never teach anything important during the last period of the day," he said and paused to gaze at me. "I know because I used to cut math class to check on you, and I still got an A on every test."

My heart skipped a beat. I wasn't sure if it was because of what Justin said or the way his sexy lips moved. They tilted upward at the corners because he caught me watching.

I reminded myself to stay focused and look in his eyes instead, but he had already pressed his mouth against mine. I officially lost control over all my senses. The kiss was warm and passionate, and it stopped me from thinking of anything at all.

When he pulled back, I took a deep breath. The buzz of his Gift causing my blood to race through my veins felt familiar and comforting. "I'm still mad at you, you know," I said and smacked him, playfully, on the chest. The lovesick look on my face didn't support my words.

Feeling defiant, I turned on my heel and walked away with my chin held high. I stole a glance at Justin before turning the corner. He stood in the same spot wearing an exaggerated frown with pouty lips and sad puppy dog eyes. He was so adorable that another giggle escaped before I dashed under the metal chain that blocked an unused staircase.

Justin rounded the corner. "I know you're mad," he said, taking two steps at a time to catch up with me and grab hold of my hand. "I could tell by the silent treatment you gave me on the car ride to school this morning."

I gave him a shamefaced smile. I knew giving the silent treatment was immature. "Well, I am mad. And hurt. And offended. And I could go on," I said, mimicking his long, frowning face.

For two days now, Justin kept quiet that he'd known Prometheus wasn't Gifted. He didn't offer an apology or bring up the topic for discussion. I knew he felt guilty about not sharing it with me. It was obvious by the way he was doubling his efforts to protect me, if that was even possible.

I understood that he wasn't going to open up to me completely in one week's time. He was used to keeping secrets to himself. Still, I had a right to be mad for a few days.

We were walking across the long and dark basement hallway, but I knew he could see my face in the thin streams of light that filtered through the windows above us. This walk used to frighten me. Not anymore. I knew there were scarier things in the world than dark hallways.

Justin pulled me close again and pressed his lips gently against mine. "I'm sorry, Liv. Always have been and always will be," he whispered.

A knot in my stomach tightened at the reminder of the years of self-blame he was carrying. The truth was, I didn't need to hear his apologies. I forgave him the moment we left the Gifted Program meeting two nights ago. That's what you do when you love someone.

I put my hands on both sides of his face and looked into his sad eyes. I kissed his lips and brushed my hands down his arms until mine were intertwined with his. I would find a way to make him feel whole again, to make him realize none of this was his fault, but now wasn't the time to approach the subject.

I didn't want to talk about what came next. I wasn't ready to tell him that I planned to go on this quest alone and shoulder the pain by myself. Today, he simply needed me to be his support system. I would worry about that conversation once I figured out a plan.

I led him into the prop room and pushed him down to the couch. Then, I squeezed in behind him, wrapping my legs around his waist, and pulling his back against my chest. The mood ring he gave me shined golden yellow from my finger.

I thought back to the pep rally last fall when he pointed out the Gifted constellations in the night sky. If I was going to solve all these mysteries, Justin needed to share his knowledge. "What other things do you know about the Gifted?" I asked, treading lightly.

I felt the rise and fall of his chest in silence for a few seconds, like he was thinking of the best place to start.

"It was obvious two years ago that Prometheus was a psycho, and I needed to watch my back, but I had also discovered I could melt metal and control water. I was scared," he began.

"You were scared?" I asked, incredulous. The words slipped out before I thought them through. Justin's back straightened like I had insulted him, which wasn't my intention. Sure, he was protective, clever, and secretive, but I never thought he was afraid.

"I was scared of accidentally hurting the people I loved. I had no clue how my Gift worked. To me, it was a curse...still is."

I had never thought of it like that. Since the very first day I received my Gift, I had Jaime to share my worries. Even though Ms. Magos had selfish motives, she had provided insight and guidance for the changes in my life. I realized I had the whole Gifted Program's support from the beginning, while Justin was alone. I hugged him while I waited for him to continue.

"I thought the best way to protect everyone was to educate myself. Did you know there are tons of books in public libraries about the Gifted? You just have to know where to look," he said, looking back at me.

"I had no idea," I told him. He nodded and turned back around.

Another few seconds passed. I held him close, resting my head against his broad shoulders. I wondered what stories were written about the Gifted in the past. Was Cleopatra Gifted? Or Leonardo da Vinci? Or Michael Jordan? The thought of so many talented people with Gifts throughout history had never crossed my mind before. It thrilled me.

Apparently, Justin's research didn't cause him to have the same reaction. "I didn't like anything I read. The Meta may be controlling, but the Gifted have a bumpy past, too," he continued. I could feel his heart rate pick up.

"In every book I read, the Horus family was worse than the others. They were leaders like Elste, but they lacked a moral compass. Their values were always skewed," he said. His voice was rising with each sentence. I rubbed his arms. His body was vibrating from his Gift, and the room was darker from his blue hue.

"Horus are the best at defense, both physically and emotionally. That's why they are usually stubborn, selfish, and loners. It's one of the main reasons Elste and Horus usually hate each other," he spat out.

"Oh yeah?" I asked. "Like who? Give me an example of a Horus descendent."

"Thomas Edison. They say he carried an odd trinket in his pocket and glowed neon blue," he said.

"The inventor of the light bulb?" I asked, incredulously.

"And the electric chair," Justin added, flatly.

"Ok, he was controversial, but also brilliant. Give me another," I argued.

"Robert Oppenheimer's aura was a shocking green and he kept a shiny magnifying glass on his keychain. He was the physicist who helped invent the atomic bomb. Don't tell me that was a warmhearted invention," he growled.

"Yeah, but didn't we learn in class that he lobbied against the use of it for years after? The entire history of villains couldn't have all been from the Horus family." I couldn't bear for him to believe there was a dark mark over his head.

His whole body twisted as he turned to face me. I could see the purple bruises beneath his narrowed eyes. "That's just it. Elste are innately good, and Horus are innately evil," he whispered in a voice cold with anger and with fear.

* * * *

Chapter Ten: The Extremist

"He wanted us to destroy the Meta's supply of the mulberry elixir," Graham said matter-of-factly. Justin and I heard him arguing loudly with someone right outside the prop room in the school basement. I clicked my tongue in frustration because Graham clearly didn't understand our Gifted Program was meant to be a secret. School was out, and I hoped the sound of kids rushing from the building was enough to mask Graham's voice.

"I know he told us that, but he obviously left out the rest of the plan since he sent us to rot in Pandora instead of taking us with him," Lynn insisted as they burst into the teeny room. If they noticed me and Justin sitting on the couch wrapped around each other, neither of them cared. Graham became a green blur as he climbed up the first two steps of a hand ladder unnecessarily fast, Lynn plopped down on a pile of newspapers and perfumed the room with her autumn apple scent, and then they both continued their argument.

Luca followed them in. His face reflected pain, and his purple glow brightened, momentarily. He wasn't as indifferent to see us in an intimate embrace as Graham and Lynn, but Chelsea forced him to keep moving as she came through the door behind him, flickering from view like a broken television. Cliff was the last to arrive, looking more lost, forlorn, and average than ever.

"Why do you think there was more to Prometheus's plan?" Chelsea asked, taking a seat on a pile of brown boxes next to Lynn and butting into their argument.

"He knew the Meta was coming the night Olivia showed up at his door with her proud band of naïve followers, no offense." Lynn didn't look at all apologetic for insulting Chelsea and her allegiance. "Don't be fooled, the split between the two groups—half sent to the Meta and half to Pandora—wasn't an accident. He knew what cards to play in order to get what he wanted," Lynn explained to Chelsea while she crossed her arms. "I just can't believe I didn't see it coming."

"If his plan wasn't to lead the Meta to his doorstep in order to get a free ride to their prison, then why come up with the Pyramus and Thisbe story? There are other ways to anger the Meta," Chelsea asked.

"Exactly my question," Lynn responded and eyed Chelsea like she was mildly impressed with her analysis. Chelsea smiled proudly, and I realized the two looked like twins with their long blonde hair, piercing blue eyes, and matching silver headbands. I wondered why I never noticed it before.

I sat up straighter, preparing myself for an hour of madness. I wasn't surprised our meeting had started abruptly and without proper order. I refused to let that unsettle me. I would try hard to decipher all the knowledge they could impart. Time was ticking and soon I would need to go at it alone.

I narrowed my eyes in concentration. Chelsea was right. My carefully-planned marriage to Justin was dropped as soon as the Meta showed up. If Prometheus really wanted to get his army inside, it might have been smarter to surprise attack them rather than be brought in as prisoners.

"Of course...," Lynn began with an evil glint in her eye. "We could ask the person who came up with the tragic Pyramus and Thisbe plan." She cocked her head accusingly towards Luca. "I think you know who it is."

Luca looked horrified. His mouth hung open as his eyes pleaded with Lynn. I felt anger bubble in my gut. Was this another secret about Prometheus that Luca decided not to share? "Who came up with the idea of creating a new Pyramus and Thisbe?" I demanded. They didn't know it yet, but I was the only one who would be fighting the Meta in the end. I refused to be played for an uninformed fool.

Luca stared at me, looking frustrated and guilty. "I was trying to tell you...I wanted to tell you...you have to understand...," Luca faltered. He turned to Lynn and gave her a look of contempt. Then, he leaped out of his seat and bounded out of the room.

"What's going on?" I asked the group that had suddenly gone silent. I got out from behind Justin and followed Luca.

In the dim hall, I watched Luca rub his temples and pace the length of the floor. What could he possibly have to tell me that would make him this nervous? I knew he would never invent the terrible tale. I walked up to him.

"Liv," he said, reaching down to hold my hand within both of his own large warm hands. They were comforting, and I bit my lip trying to hold back feelings I knew I shouldn't be feeling. "You have to believe me when I tell you that I wasn't purposely keeping anything from you. There were loyalties created before I ever met you."

He brought my hand up to his chest, resigned and ready to tell me something difficult. I caught a glimpse of Justin's mood ring. It was a dull yellow, not quite reaching the brightness it usually becomes when I am with Justin.

"Grief can drive a person to the edge of sanity. When the Meta began attacking the Gifted in the United States, people weren't scared like they are today. They didn't cower in fear and throw up their hands in defeat. They fought back. They banded together as rebels with a common target.

He stood up taller, proud of the Gifted from the past. "They had nothing left to lose. They were extremists, fighting the big bad government with every ounce of anger and strife. They spent all their time and energy plotting against the enemy." His voice was filled with passion. His eyes were wide as he tried to express the desperate urge they had to fight.

"Leaders of the movement popped up across the country, speaking their minds, uniting Gifted, and not worrying about the consequences. However, one by one the Meta captured these leaders and quieted their following," he said. Something about the angry way he said it, like he knew how it felt to be overwhelmed with fury and on the verge of madness, made me uncomfortable.

"All, except one leader who stood out as more smart and cunning than the rest. It's the same leader who came up with the Pyramus and Thisbe plan and the only person my grandfather felt safe sending me to when my parents disappeared," he finished and paused to let the information sink in.

"That leader was Evelyn Forte."

* * * *

Chapter Eleven: Gotta Have It

"Concentrate, Olivia," the middle-aged, overweight Driver's Ed instructor warned me as he stamped on the car's extra brake pedal to stop us from rolling past a stop sign and into a busy intersection.

With a late birthday, I was the last of my friends to take the Driver's Ed course. I wanted to pass, badly, but concentration on normal teenage goals was proving difficult. My emotions were erratic.

"Sorry!" I screeched and turned around to apologize to the other students grasping the car's interior from the backseat.

"Eyes front, Olivia," the instructor told me. There was a hint of frustration in his voice.

Between Justin's profession that Horus were controversial, and even evil, people, and Luca's admission that Aunt Ev came up with the Pyramus and Thisbe plan, I was wracking my brain for some sort of comforting conclusion. Bits of information kept popping to the surface like carbonation in a can of soda. I couldn't put the conversations out of my head, and my driving skills were suffering because of it.

It was hard to believe sweet Aunt Ev came up with the sinister plan to choose an innocent girl and boy and curse them into a forbidden love. Aunt Ev was always kind and welcoming. She did a good job of hiding decades of pent-up resentment. How could a sweet old woman like Aunt Ev be so menacing? I was glad she stayed in Utah when we were sent back to Pandora, but my stress levels were through the roof. Just thinking of her scared me. What else was she capable of?

I absentmindedly turned the wheel. I had analyzed my current situation from every angle possible, wondering if it was supposed to play out another way. Every time I came to the same place. Receiving my Gift, becoming an Elste, falling in love with Justin, none of it was a mistake. I could feel it in my bones.

"Keep your hands at ten and two, Olivia," growled the instructor from the seat next to me.

Now that I had validated my past, I needed to figure out my future. The only thing I knew for sure was I was powerful and supposed to finish this trek alone. What was there to be scared of? Evelyn Forte wasn't young anymore. Mr. Dimon wasn't Gifted. And Prometheus wasn't young *or* Gifted!

I closed my eyes and felt my confidence and my Gift build throughout my body. The car filled with my rose scent. I was part of a new generation. No, I was the *leader* of a newer, smarter, and stronger Gifted generation.

"Pay attention, Olivia!" the instructor yelled. He was no longer sparing my feelings or hiding his anger. "Pull into the school. Today's lesson is over."

Despite my teacher's dismay at my horrible driving skill, I felt a sudden excitement as I gathered my books and stepped out of the car. I headed towards the school with my head held high. I didn't need to learn how to drive a car to defeat the Meta.

"Hey, Liv!" Two girls from my Driver's Ed class spoke in unison as they stepped in my way and cut off my train of thought. They were far too chipper after the ride from hell that I put them through. They positioned themselves in my path and stood playing with their hair, attempting to look innocent.

"Hi, Robyn, hi, Lisa," I replied to each and paused to hear what they had to say. They were gossipy girls, and when they exchanged glances without saying a word, I decided to keep walking. I didn't want them to ruin the burst of confidence I found.

Lisa grabbed my arm to stop me, and I eyed her, suspiciously. She looked panicked for a split second and pulled her hand away, like I was contagious.

Robyn gave Lisa a pointed stare and then jumped in to save the awkward moment. "Olivia, we heard that you recently came into certain...powers," she said, whispering the last word. I stared at her and kept my face blank. What did they know? How did they find out?

Lisa and Robyn exchanged nervous glances again. "You know, something that makes guys fall in love with you," Lisa pressed on. They looked at me expectantly.

I waited another second, and then I smirked. I felt the same rush of power I felt in the car earlier. I was interesting to them. They wanted something that I had. It was a strange and new sensation, being the cool and popular girl.

Who cares if they knew I was Gifted?! I was the female Elste. I could do anything I wanted. Who would stop me?

"You mean my ability to charm?" I asked, arrogantly, and pushed between the two of them and into the school. I was enjoying the fact that they wanted to be like me. I smiled when I heard their footsteps behind me.

"Olivia!" they shouted as they followed me inside. I didn't slow my pace, letting the smell of roses drift in my wake.

I was wrapped up in the idea of being the "it" girl when I turned the corner and ran straight into Cliff. Both of my hands landed on his chest. "Liv, I need to talk to you," Cliff said and grabbed both my arms to steady me.

I looked back at Lisa and Robyn, who had gone silent. Their jaws hung open as if they had just witnessed my unique ability. I couldn't help laughing.

Cliff ignored the girls and pulled me into an empty corridor. "Liv, you need to help me. I'm dying," he said. His face was stone serious.

"Anything you need. What's wrong?" I asked, snapping out of my brash mood. Cliff and I had been through a lot this year. I was happy to call him a close friend. If there was something he wanted from me, I would give it to him.

"I need to save Helen," he told me.

My confidence deflated, and reality set in again. I still didn't know how to save my friends. "Yes, I know. I'm doing everything I can. We don't want to anger the Meta by breaking Mr. Dimon's rules. If we dig for information or leave Pandora, they might take it out on Helen. To top it all off, we don't even know where they are keeping her!" I ended on an hysterical note, throwing my arms in the air, all self-assurance rushing out of me. Cliff nodded his head, enthusiastically.

"Why are you nodding? I don't have a clue what I'm going to do!" I exclaimed.

Cliff put his hands on my shoulders. "I told you, *I* need to save Helen. It has to be me, and I have a plan. I'm sick of waiting around and feeling useless. I'm ready to take action," he announced. He looked hopeful and poised.

"Well, what's your plan?!" I asked.

"I'm going to become Gifted," he stated.

I stared at him. "What?"

"If I could just be fast like Graham or invisible like Lynn, I know I could save Helen," he said.

My eyebrows rose with concern. "Cliff...," I began. I cringed because I knew my voice sounded full of pity.

"Come on, Olivia. Don't look at me like that," Cliff said and dropped his arms. "Maybe I have a Gifted gene to be an Ikos or a Horus, but my Crescent forgot to give me jewelry."

I knew sitting on the sidelines was hard for him. I had the same unsatisfying conversation with Helen when she begged me to practice my Gift on her. She had insisted that one day she would be able to block it, but it never happened. "Becoming Gifted isn't something you plan, Cliff," I told him, trying to be gentle. "It would have happened by now. You're not supposed to be Gifted."

Angry and resolute, a fire burned in his eyes, and I stepped back instinctively. "I'm not giving up," he said and stalked away from me.

I sighed. "Neither am I," I whispered to his retreating back.

* * * *

Chapter Twelve: Before Me

Mom lingered at the door to my room. Her body movements were cautious and hesitant, but there was a confidence in her stare. Her eyes posed the questions her lips were too scared to ask: Are you in trouble? What are you hiding from me? Why don't you trust me?

I watched her stand there, curiously. I wished her warm embrace and soothing words could protect me. I felt my mouth dip into a pout, ready to collapse into a heavy sob. I was so close to breaking down and telling her everything, and then she glanced down at a box clutched to her chest, and nodded, like she received one of the answers she was looking for.

Sitting down on the bed, she clung to the box clasped between her hands. I pushed aside the homework I was working on and joined her on the bed.

"What's going on, Mom?" I asked, eying the box. The way she held it made me uneasy. I folded my hands in my lap to hold myself back from reaching out and crying in her arms.

"I want to show you something," she replied, revealing the worn edges of a greenish blue rectangle.

The box was larger than a wallet, but smaller than a pencil case. It looked aged and the word "Tiffany's" was inscribed in a delicate script across the top. Right below were the initials "J & S."

"What is it?" I asked.

She opened the tattered box, carefully. Inside was a used deck of cards in the same color as the box, and inscribed with the same details. "This deck of cards was my parents'," Mom explained. "I want to show you what I found inside."

She picked up the deck and sifted through the cards until she landed on a rectangular paper of a different thickness. I watched her pull out an old sepia photograph. Again, she held the picture close before nodding to confirm it was the right thing to do, and then she handed me the photo.

I gently held the corners of the picture between my fingers. The paper wasn't glossy like the photographs from today. The edges were frayed and browned. I was careful not to crease it.

And then I saw it. It was unmistakable. My Gifted charm necklace hung around the neck of the young woman in the photograph. She stared back at me with a slight smirk that didn't fit with her tight bun and high neckline of the time. She must have lived one hundred and fifty years ago.

"Who is she?" I asked, without taking my eyes off the picture.

"Hannah Rogers was your great-great-great-great-grandmother. Born in the 1820s, she lived in New York when women were not considered equals to men," Mom recited, like she had heard the story told the same way many times before or read it in a text book.

Her voice became deeper. "She was quick friends with ladies like Susan B. Anthony and Elizabeth Cady Stanton. They attended all the suffragist conventions, fighting for women's right to vote." Mom looked proud and whimsical. It reminded me of a look I often saw on Chelsea's face.

I was awed. I recognized the names of the other women from Global Studies class. It was strange to find out one of my relatives took part in our history. Why didn't we learn about her in class?

Mom continued in a more relaxed manner, "I remember my Great-Grandma…Nana…telling stories. Apparently, Hannah had a knack for drama when she was younger. Nana would call you 'Hannah' if you were acting up. It was the running joke in the family.

"If I remember Nana's stories correctly, Hannah was a mastermind at children's games, never lost a match, cats and dogs followed her around the house, and somehow she convinced her baby brother to do all her sewing chores," Mom shared with a smile.

She breathed in. "Cinnamon. Every time it smelled like cinnamon, Nana would mention Hannah. It was the like the smell was linked with the woman." Mom's smile grew even wider. I couldn't force my lips to join her. I wanted to scream. Hannah and I shared more than timeless jewelry. We shared a Gift.

Mom stared at my frozen face. The smile disappeared. "Despite her talent for dramatics, she took a back-seat later in life. She cared greatly for her passions, especially equality. However, others stood in the spotlight while she cheered from the sidelines."

I couldn't look in her eyes. I was afraid I might cry. Why did Hannah step back? She was a powerful female Elste. I knew it. Was I destined to do the same thing? Would others take on my cause?

Mom broke the silence. It seemed like she was following my thoughts even though I didn't say them out loud. "After this photograph, Hannah shows up in pictures without the necklace."

I sucked in a gasp of air. The chain yanked down hard against the back of my neck. Where did the necklace go for one hundred and fifty years?

"Where did you get that necklace, Olivia?" Mom asked, cautiously.

I jumped to my feet. "This necklace? I told you, it was a gift. Couldn't possibly be the same one," I told her and screwed up my face to show I believed it was impossible. I could see Mom didn't believe it for a second.

"Err...I have to go...uh…call Chelsea," I lied and got up to escape from Mom's prying eyes. She reached out her arms to me, and I felt a stab in the chest.

"Olivia, wait," Mom begged me. I had no choice. I had to go. I heard her gasp as I passed by, and I knew she smelled my Gifted rose scent.

* * * *

Chapter Thirteen: Trust Me

Mr. Rowling licked his pointer finger and used the moist end to count five sheets of paper from the top of the stack. Then he passed them to a brown-haired girl sitting in the first row. A few moments later, my copy landed on my desk. In bold letters across the top was the title of Martin Luther King, Jr's speech, "I Have a Dream."

I smoothed the ends of my hair between my fingers, dwelling on my personal drama rather than Mr. Rowling's assignment. I managed to put my mom and Hannah Rogers in the back of my mind, but now I couldn't stop thinking about Luca and his deceit. For weeks, he had information that could help us save our friends, and he kept it to himself. I needed to be able to trust Luca, but he wasn't making it easy.

"King was a master of literary and rhetorical devices. His word choice matched the strength of his message," Mr. Rowling explained to the class, beginning his lesson. I continued to play with my hair and brood over Luca's avoidance of the truth. "Olivia, can you give us an example of a literary term King used in his speech to help spread his message?" Mr. Rowling asked, pulling me out of my reverie. I could feel everyone's eyes on me. I might be able to inflict intense pain and send people to their knees, begging for mercy, but getting called on in class still caused my heart rate to speed up. I brought my hand to my necklace, instinctively.

I dug for an answer to Mr. Rowling's question, but all I could think of were Gifted problems. I had no idea what he was asking. Unfortunately, I knew he wouldn't let me pass on the question. "Err...the...err...ability to charm," I said, quietly. It was the only thing I could think of. The classroom erupted in laughter. I could feel my face flush.

Mr. Rowling waited for his students to quiet down. "In a way, that is correct. King was hoping to charm the crowd or rally the people, which he emphasized using parallelism.

"Go back to Mississippi, go back to Alabama, go back to South Carolina, go back to Georgia, go back to Louisiana, go back to the slums and ghettos of our northern cities, knowing that somehow this

situation can and will be changed," Mr. Rowling chanted to the class and accented each line with vigorous hand gestures.

It was an interesting example, and it sparked my curiosity. Was Martin Luther King Jr.'s use of literary tools and his ability to charm the masses linked to a Gift that Derek and Luca also had a knack for?

The bell rang, and the day's lesson was forgotten. I jumped out of my seat, relieved that the class was over. I looked across the room. All I wanted to do was discuss Luca's secrets with Chelsea.

I zeroed in on her huddled in the back corner with Lynn, their blondes head close together. It was strange to see Lynn close to anyone. I didn't like the way she became quick buddies with Chelsea. After the damage she caused me and my brother without showing any remorse, I had a hard time believing she only wanted to be friends with Chelsea.

I walked over and gave them a tentative smile.

"So you put two and two together?" Lynn asked. I stared at her blankly, hugging my books in my arms.

"Martin Luther King Jr. was an Elste. They say he glowed golden when he gave speeches and always carried around a shiny metal peace symbol. He put his Gift to good use, working towards freedom and civil rights." Lynn said like it was obvious. Then, she eyed me as if wondering if I would live up to the Elste family name. I didn't say a word. Chelsea and Lynn exchanged a knowing glance.

I was suddenly frustrated with the two of them. Chelsea was my friend first. "Can I talk to you for a minute?" I asked Chelsea, not caring if it was rude to exclude Lynn.

"Sure," Chelsea replied. I didn't look in Lynn's direction.

"I can tell when I'm not wanted," she said, rolled her eyes, and walked away.

Chelsea crossed her arms and asked, "What's so secretive you can't say it in front of Lynn? She's on our side!"

I wasn't so sure, but I didn't tell her that. Instead, I adjusted the books in my arms. She clicked her tongue in frustration, and waited for me to explain.

"I wanted to talk to you about Luca," I told her, however I already regretted bringing it up.

"Is this is about your ridiculous love triangle?" she asked without looking up from packing up her books.

It was at times like this I missed Helen. She would have understood, immediately. Still, I knew Chelsea would help me if I needed her. I kept my feet planted.

"Did you ever notice Luca tends to withhold useful information? He means well, but he always does the wrong thing," I said.

She looked up from packing her books and stared at me like I had just announced something obvious, like the sky was blue. "He's the other Elste in the original Pyramus and Thisbe story," she said, matter-of-factly.

"What do you mean?" I asked.

"You know, Pyramus comes back from fighting in the Gifted War. He goes to meet Thisbe in the garden, but before he reaches her, a hidden Elste kills him. An Elste who knew all their secrets," she said, dismissively.

"That's right! An Elste kills Pyramus!" I shouted slightly louder than I meant to. "What does that have to do with Luca?" I asked, lowering my voice.

"Luca is the other Elste. He knows all the secrets," she explained. I gave her a confused look.

"Luca has the same internal battle as the Elste in the story, unsure of what is right or wrong. If you lived through the first Gifted War and knew the forbidden union was about to happen again, you might be torn about what to do, too," she said. I was speechless. I remembered Pyramus was killed, but I never thought about who killed him, and why he did it.

Killing was a drastic decision, but if it saved thousands of innocent lives, perhaps it was worth it. Would Luca sacrifice my happiness for the sake of others?

Chelsea didn't give me time to process it. She grabbed my elbow and led me into the hallway. "We have bigger problems than Luca's moral compass. Apparently, the Meta is spreading propaganda to scare everyone," she told me.

I didn't understand why she was so concerned with the Meta's political activities. As long as our friends weren't being tortured, the Meta could preach about whatever they wanted. "Who told you that?" I asked.

"I listened to Mrs. Wolf's conversation with her sister," she explained without looking at me. It was exactly what I didn't want her to do.

"Chels, I thought you were going to stop sneaking around invisibly. It's too dangerous!" I scolded her.

I saw a renewed fierceness when she finally looked up at me. "Lynn thinks it's a good start. We think we should listen to Mr. Dimon's phone conversations, too," she said, getting strident with me. "We're like Margaret Kemble Gage, spying on the British army during the Revolutionary War," she added, dreamily.

"What are you talking about? Who is Margaret Kemble Gage?!" I asked, confused about how we got off topic.

"She was the famous Hadean who tipped off Paul Revere," Chelsea spat, defensively. She was clearly annoyed that we weren't on the same page.

I shook my head as if to clear it and get back on topic. "Why would you take Lynn's advice over mine? She's the one who used our own friend as bait. She's the one who snuck around the school starting fights between the boys, and she's the one who faked a relationship with my brother, just to screw us over!" I shouted, feeling confident because I got my point across.

Chelsea's anger turned to pity, and I realized my excuses sounded like a teenage girl holding a grudge. "Liv, I wouldn't worry about Lynn's opinion. It's the rest of the world we need to be concerned with." I wasn't sure what she was talking about, but I was overwhelmed.

"I didn't tell you the worst part. Mrs. Wolf's sister called in a panic. She was scared...," Chelsea spoke through my contemplation. She paused as if to give me time to prepare myself. "...scared of you."

I stared at Chelsea, struggling to comprehend what she was saying.

"The Meta issued a state of emergency warning. It claimed you are extremely dangerous. It doesn't matter that people know you, and know you're not dangerous; they will ignore logic and become irrational. Soon, the world will be terrified of the only female Elste. I'd prefer you don't meet an end like Martin Luther King Jr's."

* * * *

60

Chapter Fourteen: Freaks

A meaty hand grabbed my shoulder from behind, spun me around, and shoved me against the wall of grey lockers. The force was so strong that my head banged against the metal and black tunnel vision threatened my view.

I flung my arms around, haphazardly, but my attacker pressed his forearm into my rib cage. "Where is he?" hissed a deep male voice. He kept his face so close to mine that I could smell his last cigarette on his breath.

Panic bubbled up inside of me. Did someone break the deal with Mr. Dimon? Was this how the Meta was going to capture me, out in the open and dragged away by my hair?

I gulped for air and tried to clear my head, but he held me in place. "Who?" I asked in a strained voice. I could feel beads of sweat forming on my brow.

He shouted, "Max!" and emphasized it by thrusting his fist into my shoulder. Max? A Meta agent wouldn't be looking for Max. They already have him! The stars started clearing from my vision. I recognized the stubbly chin, thick build, and stubborn demeanor of my accuser. He was one of Max's buddies from the smokers' corner. Despite the sharp pain in my head, I felt relieved. The Meta wasn't coming to lock me up and throw away the key...yet.

I was fairly certain my brawny attacker's name was Dave. I was also pretty confident he never said a word to me when Max and I were dating, and therefore, I didn't think he would listen to a word I had to say now. I looked around for Chelsea. We had only left Mr. Rowling's class seconds earlier. She picked a great time to go invisible.

Dave was growing impatient. "My father told me he's never coming back because of you!" He shouted in my face, spraying me with spit.

"Dave," I said, trying to keep my voice calm as I attempted to pry his fingers from my shirt, "you know better than anyone else, I don't have any special tricks to force Max to do what I want..." My voice trailed off because I realized I was lying.

I glanced over Dave's shoulder and noticed his gang hovering, anxiously. Something was strange. They didn't seem pumped up to witness a fight. Was it obvious I was going to lose, and they felt bad for me? Or maybe they felt awkward watching Dave break down about his missing friend?

Perhaps it was my nerves imagining it, but some of them looked scared. It wasn't because they were worried that Dave would turn around and beat them up next. No, they were scared of me.

Chelsea finally reappeared with Lynn. I could smell vanilla and apple as they pixelated into view behind Dave's gang. "Get your hands off her," Chelsea threatened. Dave looked over his shoulder and gave a sarcastic laugh.

"Oh yeah? Which one of you dumb blondes is going to make me?" he asked. Chelsea and Lynn stared him down with their piercing blue eyes.

"Olivia, you can handle him," Lynn ordered.

Dave gave a sinister laugh and jeered, "Yeah, do it." He was putting on a convincing tough guy act, but close up I could see his mouth quiver and beads of sweat forming on his forehead. He knew what I was capable of. He wanted me to use my Gift and prove to his friends I was a monster.

I bit my lip, hesitating. "His dad knows who I am," I told them, hoping they understood my cryptic comment about being the female Elste. I looked at the crowd gathering. Whether or not people knew I was Gifted, the hallway was full of students watching intently. If I used my Gift, I would only be helping the Meta spread awful rumors about the terrifying female Elste.

Luckily, I didn't have to. There was a flash of green light. Before I could do anything else, Graham had Dave's cheek pressed against the wall and his arms behind his back.

"Why don't you mess with someone your own size?" Graham asked. His face was lit with excitement. It was the same battle-ready buzz he had shown in Prometheus's Fort Bliss and at our meeting in Ms. Magos's secret room. For once, I was happy to see it.

"Okay, you win, Thor! Get off me!" Dave yelled. He struggled against Graham's inhuman strength. Graham laughed, released him, and stepped away gracefully like he had been restraining a kitten instead of a six-foot man.

Before turning and leaving, Dave spit on the ground in front of me and growled, "Gifted freaks."

* * * *

Chapter Fifteen: Lunch

From time to time, I will admit when I'm wrong. As I rubbed my shoulder where Dave jabbed his fist, I knew this was one of those times. I couldn't deny Chelsea stood up for me, and Graham scared Dave away. It was solid proof they were on my side. If they weren't, they would have left me to fend for myself.

After listening to their insistence on retaliation and offensive strategies, I admitted their allegiance, but that didn't have to mean I had to like their style. Patience and thoughtful analysis of what happened was the way I liked to function, not action in the red heat of the moment.

We walked to the cafeteria in an absurd formation. I was the victim in protective services surrounded by her three bodyguards. Chelsea, Lynn, and Graham checked every passing person and corner before we proceeded. It was truly a ridiculous precaution since I could stop any attacker dead in their tracks before they laid a finger on me. Still, I was happy to be surrounded by friends.

Dave's outrage freaked me out. Just yesterday after Driver's Ed, I was feeling pretty good about the world knowing I was Gifted. I guess Robyn and Lisa's reaction wasn't how everyone was going to react.

We spotted Cliff sitting at a table in the corner by himself and walked over to join him. He didn't even look up and greet us. However, the rest of us sat down at the table and seemed to relax.

The calm was short-lived. I had barely unwrapped my peanut butter and jelly sandwich when the energy surrounding me started to tingle again. Justin and Luca burst through the cafeteria doors.

Both guys hustled to our table, looking worried and concerned. It was a day for proving loyalties. For the first time since they met, they were on the same side. I should have been happy about that, but I was going to feel the brunt of their panic and over-cautious plans.

They threw their book bags on the floor, grabbed chairs from the table beside us, and squeezed between Lynn and Chelsea to sit next to me.

"I'm sorry I wasn't there in time, Liv," Justin apologized. His whole face was screwed up in agony, as if it was torturing him that he was late to walk me to class. "I would have been there if someone hadn't asked the teacher a million questions and held up the whole class as the bell was ringing." His eyes turned to slits as he turned towards Luca.

Luca looked livid. "Maybe she wouldn't need a personal body guard, if you let her defend herself. She's more powerful than all of us combined!" he shouted.

Chelsea cut them off, "Before you say anything more or hover around unnecessarily, take a good look at Olivia. She's perfectly healthy and in one piece."

"I don't hover," Luca said, defensively. He moved his chair back an inch to prove a point. I smiled gratefully at Chelsea. She returned my smile. Justin didn't say a word. Instead, he placed his arm around the back of my chair, with an obvious intention to protect me from whatever came.

I sighed because I knew in the end, my friends wouldn't be able to help me. Their Gifts were susceptible to the mulberry elixir, and mine was not. I needed to face the Meta on my own. Justin was never going to accept my fate.

"Thank you, Graham," I said, turning towards him. His eyes widened in surprise. "For protecting me from Dave," I explained. He shook his head, dismissively, as if it was no big deal. He continued to devour his cheeseburger.

"Seriously, you were fast," Chelsea added.

"Like Usain Bolt," Lynn spoke, approvingly.

"Who's that?" I asked.

"Fastest Ikos ever," Graham said, in awe of the compliment.

"And a famous runner who's won about fifty gold medals in the Olympics," Luca added, impressed.

The successes and failures of the Gifted was intertwined with the history of leaders and celebrities I already knew. I had been told this fact before, but hearing real examples solidified it. We weren't the first Gifted to walk on the earth, and hopefully we wouldn't be the last.

"Are there any famous Kynikos?" I asked the table.

"Of course," Lynn confirmed. "How do you think Russia kept the Germans at bay in the Second World War?" She asked.

"No way, Kynikos caused the snow storms?!" Chelsea shouted, incredulously.

"And why do you think Alexander the Great couldn't cross the Alps? Another weather-related issue," Lynn explained.

Chelsea was sitting on the edge of her seat, ready to ask for another example when Graham groaned. He glanced over my shoulder, fleetingly, and then ducked his head. I could tell something was up when he put his burger down. There are few things that can get between Graham and food.

The whole table looked behind me. A stunning but menacing brunette was making her way over to our table. She wore a short tight skirt that emphasized each angry step her long tanned legs took. Her hair swished from side to side as she marched toward our table with her lunch tray clutched between her fingers. Everyone knew Lexy, a senior from the cheerleading squad.

"What did you do?" Lynn accused Graham.

"I've never seen her so angry," Chelsea added.

We all turned back to our table and attempted to act normal. Lexy's four-inch heels clicked closer. Graham ducked his head lower. "I told her I wouldn't go to the party with her tonight," he grimaced. "Apparently, people rarely turn her down."

The sound of clicking heels stopped. An eerie silence ensued as the rest of the cafeteria quieted to catch the action.

Suddenly, I felt something warm and gooey land on my head. Neon-orange macaroni and cheese slopped off Lexy's tray and dripped down my hair. I didn't dare turn around, but Justin shot out of his seat.

"Do something, Olivia!" Luca whispered, frantically.

"And risk the lives of our friends sitting in the Meta's prisons? Are you nuts?" Cliff asked, panic-stricken.

I kept my eyes glued to Justin's ring on my clenched fingers. It glowed in a vibrant red, like the blood pumping through my veins.

"You think you're Gifted?" Lexy asked, mockingly. "You're just a wannabe." She turned on her heels and strode away from our table.

Justin sat down again and helped clean macaroni out of my hair. He coddled me as if I might fall apart from all the negative attention, but I wasn't upset or frightened. Instead, Dave and Lexy's actions had motivated. I wanted to clear up the misconception that I was the enemy.

It was hard to believe she thought I was the reason Graham turned her down. After my incident with Cliff in front of the girls from Driver's Ed, and the information Dave angrily shouted in the hallway, it was obvious the Meta worked their propaganda quickly. Who knew the extent of the rumors that were spreading about me and my Gifted charm?

"I'm sorry, Olivia. I'll talk to her," Graham said and leaned over to pull a piece of macaroni out of my hair.

I shook my head. "Don't worry about it." Then, an idea came to me. "No, I have a better idea. We're going to that party."

Everyone stared at me like I had said I wanted to try out for the football team.

* * * *

Chapter Sixteen: Party's Over

"I can't believe we're going to this," Chelsea complained from the back seat of Justin's silver Accord. "Dave tried to turn you into a punching bag because his deadbeat father told him you were evil, and you want to greet him at the senior party."

Towards the end of every school year, the seniors throw a pre-graduation party. The location is always a secret and disclosed an hour before it begins so that teachers and parents don't ruin the fun. We were only juniors, but Cliff's buddies on the baseball team shared the location.

From the front seat I shook my head. "A jock party is the last place anyone from Max's crew would be. Plus, I'm not scared of Dave."

"Yeah," Cheslea said, "because you finally realized Lynn and Graham will protect you."

In a way, she was right. I hadn't believed they would come to my defense. Their history of deceiving me was too strong of a reason for me to fully trust them, but their actions this afternoon changed things. There was no denying it. They were a part of the plan.

Chills crept up my spine as we drove up to the original and decrepit Pandora High School. It was the location of this year's party. Ghostly as it seemed, it made me think about my quiet, even trivial, life a year ago.

Everything had changed. I couldn't go back to the way things were.

There was a reason I wanted to go to this party. If people were going to see me differently than how they saw the shy girl who barely raised her hand in class, then I wanted to be the one to reinvent my image. I didn't want someone to decide my fate for me, especially if that someone worked for the Meta.

I turned around to look at Chelsea. "You didn't see Dave's friends' reaction. I need to know if people are scared of me."

"And then what are you going to do? Charm them into liking you?" she countered.

"No," I responded and turned forward in my seat. "I don't know," I added under my breath. It would be hard to persuade people that I wasn't dangerous when I wasn't sure myself.

"Maybe I can talk to a few people," Cliff chimed in from the backseat next to Chelsea. "You know, listen to the gossip. Maybe someone knows where the Meta is."

He sounded more hopeful than he had in days. No one had the heart to tell him not to get involved in our Gifted drama. Even Justin, who usually played the part of overprotective best friend, remained silent.

Justin parked the car on a dark street a block away. Lynn and Graham walked down the block to meet us. The decision to act and move toward a goal, rather than sit and discuss strategy in our Gifted Program meetings, excited them. Joining up with Lynn and Graham brightened Chelsea's mood while it paled mine. I had wanted to go to the party under the radar rather than make an entrance with a following of angry Gifted.

As soon as the six of us were in whispering range, there was a heated battle of strategies and best ways to give the Meta what they deserved. Lynn and Graham—and now Chelsea—were never afraid to share their two cents. I turned away from the conflict. Their insistence that their plan was foolproof and the best we'd come up with was driving me crazy.

I felt Lynn's hand grab my shoulder. "Olivia, I need to talk to you," she said, forcing me to face her. Reluctantly, I let her turn me.

"What is it, Lynn?" I asked, not bothering to hide my impatience.

"It's Derek," she said. Her voice caught. She cleared her throat and adjusted the strap of her bag on her shoulder.

Her uncertainty and worry were strange behavior. I straightened, and gave her my full attention. "What about him?" I asked, forcefully. I didn't mean to snap at her, but it was my defense mechanism when it came to her.

She shook her head and looked down at the ground. "I don't know. I slipped into Mr. Dimon's office after school. I heard him talking on the phone. He mentioned your name a few times in a hushed conversation." She began pacing in front of me, holding her head with both hands.

"Then, he got upset with the person on the other end. He said something about not being able to hold us much longer." Her arms dropped to her sides. She looked right at me. "Then he said, 'Don't! Not her brother!' He sounded desperate, but the person he was talking to hung up without hearing him out." She was completely distraught. Panic stung me. I didn't know what to say.

"Olivia, what do we do?" she pleaded. It was the first time she had looked to me for answers.

I choked down my worst fears and said, "He's right. He won't be able to hold us back anymore. When I'm done with him, he won't remember what happiness is." The threat was empty without filling in the details we were missing. "Let's go," I commanded and marched toward the party.

The senior parking lot was blemished with debris thrown from the building when our Gifted power caused utter destruction a few months ago. I pictured the way life was before. I imagined Derek walking through the rows of cars with all his friends, and his insecure sister following in his shadow. That life was gone.

Pulled back to the present, we walked through the gates to the school grounds. The football field was pockmarked with mounds of dirt that would be used to complete the foundation of the new building. Somewhere under the rubble was Ms. Magos's secret room. It was the birthplace of my Gifted life. I refused to meet the same end, crumbling to nonexistence.

The baseball field sat between the old building and the football field. The bleachers on one side of the grounds, and the dugouts on the other, barricaded the swarm of students from the surrounding houses.

Two of Cliff's friends from the baseball team spotted us as we approached the crowds. As they staggered over, they slurred Cliff's name and confirmed they were drunk. Justin placed his arm around my shoulders.

It suddenly occurred to me that this was my first party. There had been so much on my mind I almost forgot kids would be drinking. With everyone's inhibitions lowered, coming to the party might be more dangerous than I originally thought.

I looked down at my ring, which was a purplish blue, and relaxed. I was closer to sad than angry, which meant the student body was safe from my female Elste wrath. I followed the group to

70

the pitcher's mound, and stuck my hands in my pockets. Looking around at the girls wearing short skirts and giggling with their friends, I felt a little out of place.

I spotted Luca in the dugout. An empty bottle hung loosely from his right hand. He was engrossed in a conversation with a beautiful dark-haired girl.

I felt my stomach flip. Who was she? I crossed my arms and watched them. Why did they have to sit so close that their legs touched?

Graham's booming voice brought me back to the current conversation. "Cliff, you need to live for today. Check out all the possibilities around you." He slapped Cliff on the back, and motioned to two passing senior girls wearing tight pants and low-cut shirts.

Cliff shoved his hand away. "Hey, man. That's your thing, not mine. If someone I care about needs my help, I'll figure out a way." Cliff turned on his heel and left the group. Justin groaned and went after him.

I looked back at the dugout. Luca was still sitting there, but the beautiful girl was gone. He was holding his head between his hands, so I decided to check on him. I told myself it wasn't because I needed to know who the brunette babe was, but I was definitely feeling the jealousy bug as I made my way over with my arms crossed at my chest.

The dugout smelled strongly like grass. Luca looked up at me when I approached. His eyes were watery and the bottle had been abandoned on the floor. "Olivia..." His tone pulled at my heart strings.

I hurried the last few feet and sat down on the bench next to him and wrapped my arm around his shoulders, forgetting all about the pretty girl. "What's wrong?" I asked.

"My parents...," he said, trailing off. I could smell the alcohol on his breath. I tried not to flinch as it invaded my nostrils.

"Shh, Luca. It's okay," I tried to soothe him. "What about your parents?" I pressed.

"Terrible...I'm too ashamed..."

"Luca, we're friends. Tell me what's wrong. I won't judge you," I told him, hoping I was right.

71

He looked at my face as if to determine I was sincere. "They were Meta sympathizers…or, at least, they didn't care about the Gifted…" He was babbling.

"What do you mean? What did you find out about your parents?" I asked, trying to lead him in a direction that would help explain his sorrow.

"They were suppliers," he choked out before shaking his head and hanging it low. I rubbed his back to comfort him.

"Suppliers of what? To whom?"

He raised his head again to look at me. "Suppliers of the mulberry elixir to the Meta," he told me, and I could see the pain of the words reflected in his eyes. "They had no Gifts of their own, and they liked to play both sides of their deals, not really loyal to the Gifted or to the Meta. Then, something happened and the Meta wasn't happy with them."

I was momentarily immobilized. The story irked me for many reasons, but mostly it reminded me of the other Elste in the original Pyramus and Thisbe story. "Is this another story you forgot to tell me?" I asked, trying not to sound angry.

He turned toward me, quickly, grabbing my hands and pulling me close. "No, no, no, 'Livia. I promise, I didn't know. Carly jus' tol' me. I didn't realize why my grandfather stayed away from them throughout my childhood. He was Gifted and embarrassed by my parents. I 'ad no idea," he said in a drunken slur, begging me to understand.

"Carly from Salt Lake City is here?" I asked, beginning to realize why the dugout smelled strongly like grass. I couldn't believe I was jealous of her. I tried not to let the embarrassment faze me.

"Yes, see shaid Aunt Ev shent her here t' talk t'me." He was slurring his words.

I was suspicious of Aunt Ev's timing for sending Carly. After finding out she was a famous extremist in the Gifted community who came up with the plan to use me as a pawn against the Meta, I didn't trust her. In fact, hearing her name made me tremble.

"'Livia, tell me you aren't mad at me. I wouldn't be able to lif wif myself if you 'ated me," Luca said. The alcohol was making him sound whiny, and I was feeling extra sorry for him.

I shook my head, but before I could tell him not to worry he was crushing my lips with his own. It wasn't graceful and breathtaking like the last time. His teeth smacked against my own, and I was able to turn away before he could try again.

"Luca!" I scolded. I didn't have time to say anything else; a jarring siren went off and the entire party turned into disarray.

* * * *

Chapter Seventeen: Take Responsibility

The blaring sirens were a wake-up call. My friends were constantly in danger as long as I was near. It was time to go. Time to set off on my own against the Meta. If I left now, no one would stop me.

I could do it. I was the female Elste. The next time I was threatened by someone like Dave or worse, I would defend myself. I wiped my sweaty palms on my jeans. Then why was I standing still?

I took an uneasy step out of the dugout and sank into the shadow. I felt nothing like the powerful Thisbe. I felt average. I stood there, hoping it would pass and a wave of courage would overtake me.

Instead, I heard Luca's ragged breathing. Each intake of air begged me to step back into the light. My friends would think I was captured by the Meta. How could I live like that?

Then I heard Justin. "Olivia! Olivia! Where are you?" He was screaming from the pitcher's mound. The panic was unmistakable. He must have known my plan along, and thought I had already left him.

Now that I was paying attention, I saw the party was pure chaos. Football guys were staggering off the field. Couples were coming out from behind bushes. Cheerleaders were grabbing their friends and disappearing into getaway cars.

I kept my eyes on Justin. He frantically scanned the passing people, all purpose and meaning draining from his soul. That one look was all I needed to change my mind. One look confirmed I was the center of his life, and he was the center of mine. I would never go on without him.

"Justin! I'm okay. I'm over here!" I shouted back. I watched the relief on his face, and my heart skipped a beat.

Luca stirred at the sound of my voice. He let out a groan, and I realized I could never leave him either. He wasn't my center, but he was my support. I began pacing the length of the dugout. Luca was too drunk for me to direct him where to go.

Justin rushed over to us. "Help me!" I said, motioning to Luca who was slumped at the end of the bench. Justin gave me a look of disbelief. When I didn't change my adamant expression, he threw Luca's arm over his shoulder and lifted him to his feet.

The sirens blared louder and louder sending everyone into a frenzy. Cops stormed the field from all the entrances.

I hadn't drunk a single sip of alcohol, but I couldn't help feeling like I had done something wrong. That was why I felt a jolt of panic when a state trooper cornered Justin, Luca, and me. He was over six feet tall and wearing a wide-brimmed hat that kept his face in the dark. Being unable to see the whites of his eyes was intimidating.

"You three are coming with me," he declared and grabbed Justin by the collar of his jacket.

"Excuse me, sir, we're trying to get our sick friend home," I attempted and sent him my most innocent-looking smile.

Perhaps it looked more like a grimace because the trooper glared at me and said, "I know what you are, Miss Hart, so don't try any funny business." The way he snapped and adjusted the gun on his hip made me think he knew about my Gift. There was definitely something fishy. I decided to follow his instructions without question.

Sitting inside a locked state trooper's car and behind metal bars, made me feel, once again, like a caged animal. After an uncomfortable ride, we stopped in front of Justin's house. I reached across Luca, who had passed out in the middle seat, and squeezed Justin's hand. He looked frightened and unwilling to leave me alone. I leaned back in my seat to prepare for the next stop.

"Everybody out!" the state trooper ordered. Everybody? Justin and I exchanged glances. Why wasn't he taking me home? I was sure my parents would have heard about the party bust and would be waiting for me.

The state trooper opened my door and motioned me to go inside the house. Justin pulled Luca out the other side of the car. Luca groaned, but we threw each of his arms over our shoulders and hurried to get inside. The state trooper didn't follow us.

Something felt strange the minute we walked in the front door. Justin's mom didn't meet us, ready to scold. In fact, most of the lights were turned off. The house usually felt warm and welcoming, but the glow of a single light coming from the den downstairs looked cold and ominous.

Again, Justin and I shared our thoughts with just a look. My heartbeat sped up as we made our way down the stairs, moving slowly and clumsily with Luca wrapped around our necks.

Peering into the room, I felt a tingling sensation creep up my spine. Sitting on the couch with her hands clasped in her lap was Great-Aunt Ev. She was wearing her usual grin with her eyebrows high on her forehead, but this time her warm welcome felt insincere. She spent years scheming and plotting against the Meta. The friendly great-aunt I met in Salt Lake City was an act, and I was only a pawn in her chess game.

I was no longer scared and powerless. My anger had officially reached a peak higher than Max's. I was irate and sick of being played as a fool. Taking one step in front of Justin and Luca, I balled my hands into fists in front of me, clenched my jaw, and felt the immense surge of my Gift from my core.

"Get. Out," I growled, enunciating each sound and glaring at the old woman. Aunt Ev didn't flinch. My Gift buzzed with a life of its own. I wasn't sure if she was unbelievably tough or implausibly suicidal.

In a voice that was both firm and gentle she said, "Olivia, darling." I dug my nails into my fists. How dare she call me *darling*!

I lurched forward, but she put her hands up. "Before you use your Elste Gift on me, I need to tell you a few things," she said and this time her voice sounded urgent.

"Ev, is that you?" Luca asked. He swayed because he was unstable. "Carly....you sent Carly," he slurred.

"Yes, I did, and if the next few days weren't important, I would ground you for this drunken behavior," she said, harshly. I kept my eyes on Aunt Ev, but I heard Luca whimpering behind me.

"Why send Carly now?" My look was accusing. "You had years to tell him the truth about his parents."

"Because we all have a dark past, sometimes from our own doing, sometimes from what our family or our ancestors did. Knowing the truth helps us heal and move forward. You all need to internalize that pain and strengthen your Gift," she told us. I wasn't sure if she was apologizing for her own actions, or Luca's parents', or for Thisbe. All I heard was the venom in her voice from her own

76

pent-up emotions. Considering she was calling all the shots, I didn't plan on softening my stance.

"Why should we listen to you? Because you are always looking out for our own good?" My sarcasm was venomous. She could feed me stories about overcoming darkness, but I wasn't ready to believe them.

"I know it may not look like that," she responded.

"You know what it looks like, Evelyn Forte? It looks like you are the ringmaster, and we are the dumb clowns in your circus. Is everyone under your control? Let me guess, the state trooper was once a member of your Gifted Retreat. I guess Prometheus was working for you, too. I wouldn't be surprised if Mr. Dimon is actually one of your cronies!" I was shouting by then.

Aunt Ev was still until I finished. "No, not everyone," she said, and turned to Justin's grandma sitting on her left. She was sitting so statuesquely that I hardly even noticed she was there until Aunt Ev looked at her.

"Do you want to tell them?" Aunt Ev asked the quiet woman.

"Yes, I think it's time," she responded.

"You speak English?" I was incredulous, and then snapped my mouth shut. Should I have been surprised? There was so much I didn't know.

Her sea foam eyes locked with mine. "I do. I prefer not to speak to people, so I use German most of the time," she told me.

"Grandma…?" Justin said her name like a warning. I took a step back and looked at my feet.

"It is time you heard this story, my love," she responded. "People often confuse me with my twin sister, someone I'm embarrassed and ashamed of. We look the same on the outside, but the real difference is on the inside. My sister is arrogant, selfish…and Gifted," she said. I bristled, but stayed silent.

"We knew nothing about our family history. Our father came to America as young boy to be an apprentice in a small printing shop. Within three months, the man who owned the shop passed away. Without money to travel back to Europe, he stayed in the United States, working whatever jobs he could find. He eventually met my mother and they married, but our mother didn't make it through our birth. Then my father found work as a janitor at a university. The

77

professors took a liking to him, and oftentimes, he was invited to stay and listen to a class.

"Chemistry was his favorite subject, and one day a professor mentioned a new agency in town that was looking for chemists. He referred my father to the group, and he started working at a subdivision of the Meta. They had opened an office in Washington D.C. to pacify the growing number of governments that blamed the Gifted for their problems.

"My sister and I lived with our father during a tumultuous social atmosphere. Being around politicians all the time, we believed all the propaganda and smut about the Gifted. Until a box came in the mail addressed to my sister from an uncle on my mother's side whom we never met. Seventeen and pregnant, my sister found a Gifted knife inside." She took a deep breath as if telling the story winded her.

"I'm not jealous because I wasn't born with the ability to change the physical components of anything I wanted. I'm angry because my sister saw it as a mark of weakness rather than a responsibility. She didn't take any pride in her Gift, and she kept it a secret. Her insecurities grew over time. She believed there was only one way to make it right. Fortunately for us, her actions never cured what she believed to be a disease," she explained. The room was still. "You see, she has made many mistakes…as the Chancellor of the Meta."

I was speechless. Justin's great-aunt was a Horus and the chancellor of the Meta. I could feel the air prickling from Justin behind me.

She looked Justin in the eyes. "That's not all. Fearing her 'disability' was contagious, she asked me to step in as a mother for her little girl, and she walked away."

I felt Justin push past me. "Is that true?" he asked her.

"Yes, I am not your biological grandmother, but I take credit for every one of your successes. When it comes to you and your mother, I refuse to apologize for the opportunity my sister bestowed on me. On top of that, I am happy to see she failed at keeping you from your Gifted identity. Of course, my father—your great-grandfather—made sure of that," she said and the corners of her mouth tipped up. "What does he like to go by these days....oh, right...Prometheus."

* * * *

78

Chapter Eighteen: The Power of Youth

I heard the front door swing open upstairs. We all froze in place as it slammed against the wall. "Don't worry, Luca! We're coming to save you!" Graham broke through our panic and screamed from the landing above. Two female voices tried to hush him.

Graham ignored their warnings. "I'm coming, Luca! Best friends for life! I won't let them tell Evelyn...," he managed to form the full sentences, even if the words were slurred, before he tumbled down the stairs in a green blur. Despite the fall, his Gifted agility was acute. He completed a perfect somersault and landed on one knee in front of Aunt Ev.

"Won't let them tell me what, Graham? That he had just as many alcoholic beverages as you?" Aunt Ev questioned him with the perfect concerned-parent look on her face.

"Evelyn! Great to see you!" Graham cooed with a brilliant change of expression, and reached up to give her a bear hug.

She patted him on the back. "We will deal with your misuse of my trust later," she warned him.

"What are we doing now?" he asked with drunken zest.

"You are going to the Meta, of course," she said, as if it were obvious.

"Says who?" Chelsea asked, coming to the bottom of the steps and surveying the room. "Judging by the angry and hurt looks on Olivia, Justin, and Luca's faces, we missed important details," Chelsea accused, not in the mood to trust anyone.

I sighed, trying to release some of the tension. "Let's see, the chancellor of the Meta is actually a Gifted Huron, who happens to be Justin's actual grandmother, and Marie's Gifted-loathing sister." There was a sarcasm in my voice I never heard before. Chelsea was speechless. "Does that sum it up, Aunt Ev?"

Aunt Ev pursed her lips together in a tight smile. "Yes, Olivia. It does," she conceded. "I know you are all frustrated and feeling used. You have to understand we never meant to hurt you," she insisted and folded her hands in her lap, settling in for a long story.

"Wait, where's Cliff?" Justin asked, looking around the room.

"He was talking to that beefy kid named Dave the last time I saw him," Lynn said. Justin looked confused, but kept quiet. Did Cliff finally get fed up with our inability to find Helen? Was he turning against his Gifted friends? Justin looked defeated, and it was disheartening to watch. I didn't want to remind him he couldn't protect everyone.

Aunt Ev took the silence as a sign to continue. "When Prometheus's oldest daughter was hired at the Meta as a clerk-typist, decades ago, the governing body was already sick of defending the Gifted from the unfounded but plentiful accusations by other governing bodies looking for a scapegoat. Weak and without a clear leader to direct them, the tone was already turning negative towards the Gifted.

"Prometheus could see how the hatred for the Gifted was changing his daughter. Her greed for power was fed by the need to hide her Gift. Fearing his time at the Meta was ending and the existence of the Gifted was at peril, Prometheus gathered Gifted jewelry from the Meta's vault.

"His own daughter ratted him out and brought back the jewelry, proving her loyalty to the Meta. Winning over her fellow employees, she was rewarded by being named Chancellor. Prometheus, on the other hand, was exiled. He knew he needed to stop her," she said, as if his path was obvious.

Looking slightly smug, she continued, "My Pyramus and Thisbe plan was well known, and he sought me out. He knew the imminent threat of power created from the union of an Elste girl and a Horus boy would frighten the Meta, which was why I was ecstatic when he brought the final piece to the puzzle." She focused on me. "An Elste necklace." I felt the chain turn ice cold around my neck.

"The Chancellor was unaware that Prometheus had managed to hang on to a few pieces of jewelry, including the necklace with a tag that read *Hannah Rogers, female Elste, confiscated 1845*," Aunt Ev explained. I felt my stomach tighten. It was true. I was wearing my great-great-great-great-grandmother's necklace.

"Prometheus didn't think it would be enough to frighten the Meta. However, he believed the exposure of the Chancellor's Gifted kin would weaken her control. It was no accident so many talented Gifted ended up in the town of Pandora. The plan was to find a descendant of Hannah Rogers, surround her with strong Gifted friends, and help her fall in love with the Gifted grandson of the chancellor of Meta. Once we found the Harts, Max's great-uncle Joe, Chelsea's grandmother's sister, Prometheus, and I each convinced our relatives to settle in Pandora as well."

My knees felt weak. The destiny of my friends was doomed before we were born, and I never had the option to free Justin of his burden. They couldn't substitute another Horus. He was chosen and condemned, just the same as I was, against our will.

Aunt Ev sighed, looking more like ninety-seven years old than usual. "We waited generations for a female to be born in the Hart family and Justin's mother to produce a son. There were years when we lost hope and years when we decided the trade off wasn't worth it.

"As a leader of the Gifted rebellion, it wasn't revenge that motivated me to dream up the re-creation of Pyramus and Thisbe. It was hope for a better future for Gifted children. Time had changed things. Our lives were different. The Gifted Retreat was a success, my sisters had families to watch over, and I had adopted children of my own," she explained, smiling at Luca.

"Although our Gifted lives were still a secret, our human lives were so full. I fought Prometheus to put an end to the plan, but he had become obsessed. Instead, he disappeared, and I believed in the illusion that our lives would end, peacefully," she said, glancing at each of us mournfully. Her haunted eyes landed on me. "Until I met the brokenhearted Elste who longed to be with her Horus, and I knew once the wheels were put in motion, there was no stopping Prometheus."

We were silent. Every emotion coursed through my body: anger, remorse, frustration. I could walk away from this crazy plan. I didn't owe Prometheus anything.

"If you didn't want him to follow through, then why did you let us go to Fort Bliss?" I asked.

She smiled, sadly. "Seeing you work together for Gifted rights reminded me of what I fought for. I didn't know he planned to send half of you to the Meta's prisons, including my great- niece, but I have to admit, it was genius. You will fight harder for your friends."

Aunt Ev was right. I couldn't back out. My friends needed me, and I wouldn't give up until they were free and safe.

"So you know where the Meta is?" Chelsea asked, bursting forward.

Aunt Ev sighed and said, "No, unfortunately. The Chancellor has always been an expert at concealing the location, but there is someone in Pandora who knows."

"Mr. Dimon," Justin said, with no inflection in his voice.

* * * *

Chapter Nineteen: Roses Have Thorns

My hand was shaking as I held the phone to my ear. Justin brushed my cheek, lightly, and I felt the beautiful buzz of his Gift warm my blood. We were sitting in his car outside the high school. The light to Mr. Dimon's office was a faint glow at the end of the brick building. We weren't surprised to find out he was still at the school, given the upheaval after the senior party.

I listened to the phone ring twice on the other line, and then I heard my mom's shrill voice, "Olivia?!" She didn't try to hide the panic. It was after midnight.

"Hi, Mom," I said. My own voice was calmer than I felt. "I'm calling to tell you I am going to see Helen."

"Tonight?! Olivia, where *are* you?" she asked.

"Yes, I have to leave tonight," I confirmed, ignoring her second question. There was silence on the other end of the phone. I waited for her list of reasons why I shouldn't go.

"Okay," she said, defeated.

Now it was my turn to be shocked. "Okay?"

Mom sighed. "I know something is going on with Helen and Derek and probably others. I also know you are at the center of it. Olivia..."

How did she know something was going on? The guilt built as I realized she knew I was keeping secrets from her. Somehow that was worse than actually keeping the secret, like when parents say they're not mad, just disappointed. I thought I was protecting her. Perhaps I was wrong. I waited while she gathered her thoughts and prepared myself to hear her concerns.

"You are mature and behave like an adult, and I don't need to tell you how to treat others or remind you to be safe. They need you to lead them. You have Hannah Rogers's spirit inside of you. I have faith in you."

She said exactly what I needed to hear. "Thanks, Mom. I love you. I'll call you," I said and hung up the phone. Something about a mother's guarantee did wonders for self-confidence. I felt hopeful because Mom said I could do it. I was going to save my friends.

I took a deep breath and looked at Justin. "I have faith in you, too," he said. He dropped his gaze, focusing on his hands in his lap. "But I don't have faith in myself. I researched every Huron, but I never looked at my own family. My grandmother is the worst Huron in modern history." He said the word 'grandmother' with disgust. "What does that mean for me?" He asked.

I reached over and held both of his hands. His sad sea foam eyes searched my own for answers. "If there's anything I learned from this experience, it's that the actions of our relatives don't define us. You need to create your own destiny, and I will help you," I promised.

Aunt Ev gave us protective gear. Long capes, thick belts, and heavy boots; it was the same fighter gear Hunter, Lynn, and Graham were wearing when they captured Helen in the fall and at Prometheus's mansion a few weeks ago. Aunt Ev insisted they would be useful as a repellent when the Meta agents were attacking us with the mulberry elixir.

In my new Gifted boots, I stepped out of the car and smoothed my silver cape. I felt the buzz of my power and raised my hand to cradle the charm on my necklace.

With Justin's long strides around the car, his silver cape billowed behind him. When his sea foam and now-resolute eyes met mine, the effect was powerful. His striking features, lean body, and strong jaw line were sexy, but more than that, he looked like a superhero.

Storming through the school's front doors, we marched the length of the hallway. Each step empowered me, and I could smell the rush of roses following in my wake. Justin was next to me. A cloud of dark blue held tight to his cape and cast a shadow on our faces like another layer of our suits.

The muscles in my body were tense because I was determined now. There was no more indecision. We had a plan, and we would save our friends.

I didn't hesitate when we reached Mr. Dimon's door. I grabbed the handle and pushed in. I felt my Gift explode into the room with me.

Mr. Dimon shot out of his desk chair. Mrs. Wolf tumbled out of his lap and on to the floor. Their hair was ruffled and their faces were pink like we interrupted an intimate embrace. I finally

85

understood why our Gifted school nurse was allowed to stay in Pandora.

Mr. Dimon's dark eyes narrowed when he saw who had barged in. "What are you doing here, Olivia?" he demanded. His voice rang with authority and the muscles of his severe jawline tightened.

Mrs. Wolf cowered in the corner. Her body was visibly shaking, and her frightened round eyes were glued to me.

I took one step forward, and he took one step back, involuntarily. I saw his white knuckles as he grasped the shelf behind him.

I smiled and said, "I guess you heard the rumors about the dangerous female Elste, too." I took another deliberate step towards him. He struggled to take a breath.

Mrs. Wolf gave out a yelp, and disappeared into a flash of pink. Inhumanly fast, she was suddenly on the windowsill, trying to pry open the glass. The metal casing groaned under her Ikos strength, but wouldn't budge. Without warning, she was another pink blur behind us, attempting to get out of the door.

Justin put one hand on her shoulder and steam escaped from under his fingers. She shouted in agony and stepped back, defeated. Mr. Dimon had watched the interaction with a dawning realization that he was the weakest in the room.

"I know you're scared," I said and leaned my hands on Mr. Dimon's desk. "And you have the Chancellor of the Meta to thank for that. I didn't fully understand my Gifted strength until she started gossiping, and if you try to run, I'll show you exactly what I mean." I paused to feel the buzz of my Gift. It twinkled around the edges of my consciousness, and then I winked at Mr. Dimon.

The second my Gift pricked him, I watched him grit his teeth and stick out his chin, stubbornly. He didn't realize I was holding back. No one else knew the power of my Gift because there was no one else like me.

"Still not going to admit you're scared? Maybe this will change your mind," I told him. Chelsea, Luca, Graham, and Lynn stepped through the door and stood next to Justin, lining the wall behind me. Mrs. Wolf leaned against the wall and sunk to the floor.

Mr. Dimon gulped. His eyes darted between us. "What do you want?" he asked in a low raspy voice.

"We want to know where they are keeping our friends. Where is the Meta?" I growled back. My hands were balled into menacing fists. The fury from the last week hit a peak. Our Gifts were at an all time high. The room was filled with smoky greens, blues, and purples and smelled like a dangerous wall of roses tinted with sickly sweet vanilla and poisonous apples.

Mr. Dimon was not Gifted, but he felt the power, too. He gave in. "Isn't it obvious? The Chancellor built the Meta in an area where she could easily control the most people. Somewhere that is teaming with so many Gifted people it creates a constant fog throughout the city," he explained and shook his head like it that made it clear. "The Meta is in San Francisco."

* * * *

Chapter Twenty: Written in the Stars

I had fallen asleep on the plane, and the vivid dream about Derek teasing me felt so real. I didn't want to wake up, but I couldn't ignore the sharp and blunt pain in my side.

I begrudgingly opened one eye and saw Chelsea wind up to jab me again with her elbow. I flinched and said, "Okay, I'm up!"

"Look outside," she ordered. I peeked over her lap and through the window. First, I saw bright stars twinkling against a black night sky. I smiled. The sparkly gems arranged in my favorite constellations looked beautiful.

Then the pilot announced we should prepare for landing, and the plane shifted. The city of San Francisco came into view. I leaned closer.

A murky cloud of fog covered the city. It hovered around a baseball field perched near the water's edge, lingered over the blanket of houses that covered nearby hills, and weaved in and out of the red cables of the Golden Gate Bridge.

"Do you see it?" Chelsea asked.

"Yeah, it's a big city," I told her.

She clicked her tongue and shook her head in frustration. "No, really look," she said.

I leaned in again and focused on the world below, not sure what she wanted me to see. I watched the fog shift and stir like a living being. In the night sky it reflected the city lights below, but something did look strange.

Squinting my eyes, I tried to see it clearer. The fog was doing more than reflecting the light below. It pulsed in vibrant blues and yellows and reds. Mixing and combining, the puffs of air were massive and covered large spans of land.

"You're seeing the other Gifted," Chelsea said and nodded towards the window. "They need our help, too. This isn't just a mission to save our friends and run. Aunt Ev is right. We have a responsibility to defend Gifted rights. And Olivia, it all falls on your shoulders. As a female Elste, you are the only one with enough power to do it."

I continued to stare out the window at the multicolored fog. It was beautiful, and it needed to be protected. I closed my eyes and imagined the whole world covered in it. Then, I took a deep breath in and thought of what that world would smell like - delicious flavors, brilliant flowers, and sweet tastes.

Chelsea got out of her seat and Carly leaned in. My jaw tightened involuntarily. I didn't know why she needed to come with us. She was young and volatile, but Aunt Ev insisted.

"That's a lot of pressure," Carly whispered, sarcastically. She enjoyed watching me squirm. I rolled my eyes and looked at her. She wasn't looking at me. Instead, she was pointing her finger at the back of the chair in front of her as if to say I wasn't important enough to give her full attention.

Besides me and Justin, she was the happiest about our rekindled romance. It meant Luca might take his attention off me and focus on Carly.

I watched a spark jump from her finger and singe a loose thread on the seat. I held back the urge to tell her to quit it and sighed. Maybe Carly wasn't bratty. The problem was she was constantly comparing herself to the female Elste.

I softened. She shouldn't feel threatened. The odds were always against me. She had no idea the pressure I felt, and the helplessness that followed me around when I didn't live up to expectations.

The seat belt sign turned off and the sound of unbuckling played throughout the plane in unison. I stood up and gathered my belongings. Aunt Ev had told us to look for an older man named Bill. She said he was an old friend who worked at the airport and would help us. That was the only instruction she gave us.

We walked off the plane in a small mob. The San Francisco airport was full of people. A row of airport workers pushing wheelchairs cut in between our group. Lynn, Chelsea, Justin, and Carly got stuck behind senior travelers who were indecisive about their next steps.

Luca hooked his arm under my elbow and stuck out an arm to stop Graham. He brought his lips to my ear and whispered, "Meta agents." The words sent a chill up my spine, and I froze in place.

I counted ten agents with bats and guns. They walked with menacing authority, looking through the throngs of people for Gifted wrongdoers. I instinctively reached for my necklace. The cocky agent on the end of the lineup swung his gun around wildly. A red sloppy liquid dripped from the end. His weapon was filled with the mulberry elixir.

"Olivia!" Chelsea shouted from behind a group of scattered people. I looked over my shoulder for her and locked eyes with a shocked hipster. I watched his baby blues lower their focus to my hand, zoning in on the shiny charm around my neck.

"It's her! The female Elste!" he screamed and pointed an accusatory finger at me.

When I gasped, the Meta agent on the end of the lineup switched his attention. The gun stopped swinging and went into ready position. I grit my teeth, took a breath, and felt my Gift flood my body. The scent of roses burst around me. Time to kick some Meta butt.

"Wait," Luca whispered. "If you get hit with the mulberry elixir and it doesn't stop your Gift, they will know it's you. Let's not confirm their suspicions. Right now, we're under the radar."

Luca was right, no one knew the only female Elste was coming, however, judging by the special care the Meta agent was taking to aim his gun, he knew we were some version of Gifted.

"We can't just stand here," I whispered back.

"I got this," Graham announced and launched forward. We watched him take two athletic quick lunges toward the agents. He unzipped the hoodie that was covering his anti-elixir getup. His arms swung swiftly at his sides to propel him, and then he was an army-green blur.

He made it to the first two agents fast enough to swat their elixir guns into the air, and I was hopeful his fighter outfit would make him unstoppable, and he could distract them long enough to escape their clutches; however the last few agents were fast.

In a matter of seconds, Graham reappeared covered in mulberry juice and no longer radiating his green Gift. Every inch of his exposed skin was drenched. His protective gear never stood a chance. The Meta agents circled him.

"RUN!" he shouted from inside the swarm of his attackers. Luca and I listened to him. We turned on our heels in the opposite direction. Catching up with Lynn, Chelsea, Justin, and Carly, we grabbed them and kept moving.

I peeked over my shoulder and saw three Meta agents turning the bend behind us. Red slime squirted in all directions, covering suitcases, walls, and travelers. My stomach jumped into my throat, but I kept running past lanky teenagers, couples with little children, and foreign tourist groups. The adrenaline rush had us all moving fast, but the trained and fit agents were gaining speed.

"Chelsea, you know what to do!" Lynn shouted. There was a hint of excitement in her voice that I would never understand. When it came to fight or flight, I always wanted to run for the hills. Luckily, Chelsea and Lynn were the opposite. Both girls slipped out of site, leaving a wake of apple and vanilla scents behind them.

I glanced back. Our pursuers kept their speed, spraying the elixir in all directions. Suddenly, one Meta agent flew headfirst like he tripped over an invisible wire, and another looked dumbstruck when he ran into and was stopped by what appeared to be an invisible wall.

One agent remained on our tail. I felt my heart beating from within my heaving chest. A puff of blue smoke billowed out from Justin as he jumped and grabbed on to an exposed pipe. Swinging back and forth, the pipe groaned and split open. He landed a few feet in front of the agent who slipped and sloshed as Justin ran forward. The agent wasn't deterred. I gasped as he moved closer.

"I'll charm them," Luca shouted and began to slow.

"No! People might confuse your charm for mine!" I screamed and urged him to keep moving. Luca, Justin, Carly, and I were frantic.

"I got it!" Carly shouted. She turned on the spot and held both arms out. Lightning erupted from her fingers and lit up the room. The ceiling burst into flames. Fiery ceiling tiles fell on the agent, stopping him cold.

A door down the hall jutted open. "In here," an older man, wearing worn sneakers and a ratty jacket, called to us. Perhaps it was the fear of being caught by the Meta agents before we even made it out of the airport, or maybe it was the innocent look on the old man's face, or it could have been that I was simply out of breath. For some reason, I trusted him, and we followed the man into the corridor.

* * * *

Chapter Twenty-One: Push

Ding. Ding. An electronic bell rang twice as the doors to the train car shut behind us. Our introduction to San Francisco was the epitome of the phrase, 'take the city by storm.' Therefore, the atmosphere was ironically low key and quiet when we boarded the Bart at the airport station a half hour later.

We might have been running from the bad guys, but the rest of the world was going about their regular day. I tried to imagine heading to work or to visit to a relative. At this point, it seemed irrational.

It was Aunt Ev's friend, Bill, who hid us from the Meta guards. There was nothing particularly memorable about him. A thinning crown of mousy brown and grey hair circled a bald spot. He had slouched as he told us we weren't hard to find. With the destruction we caused in the airport, it was no surprise we had drawn attention to ourselves.

Ensuring no one else found us was proving to be more difficult. Bill couldn't fit us all in his car, so we were taking the train. He gave us specific instructions to meet him at Coit Tower.

I focused on the short-stacked apartment buildings and bright colored Victorian townhouses we passed. I felt every dip and turn the Bart made around the famous hills of the city. I had never been to San Francisco before. I tried to keep my facial features blank so we didn't tip off anyone that something was odd.

I shouldn't have been worried. Train passengers were scattered throughout the car, and their clothing, conversations, and cultures varied, widely, making our group of high school kids appear the most normal.

Two Asian women sat behind us, chattering about organic vegetables and gluten-free pastas. An Apple Inc. security badge hung from the belt loop of the nerdy man on our right. Two men standing arm and arm near the door were wearing matching leather chaps and vests. They all appeared innocent enough, but I couldn't help checking over my shoulder every few minutes.

We had squished into an area with six seats, and I could feel the tension in the air. I looked at my ragged crew. Carly had a habit of biting her nails when she was nervous. Lynn scanned the other passengers like everyone might be the enemy. Chelsea's left hand kept disappearing, and Justin had his arm wrapped protectively around me.

Everyone was anxious, but Luca was worst of all. The rims of his eyes were red, and he bounced in his seat. I wracked my brain for something inspiring to say; something a general would tell his tattered army between battles. Lynn was right: I wasn't anything like Martin Luther King Jr. I sat there fuming at myself.

"We made a mistake," Luca announced. He was leaning in with his elbows propped on his knees.

"What do you mean?" Chelsea asked. I felt sick looking into Luca's distraught eyes. He hadn't smiled in days.

"We should have stayed together. We shouldn't have let Graham sacrifice himself," Luca said. He ran both hands through his hair, roughly. I understood how he felt. They took his best friend, just like they took Helen.

Lynn leaned in as well and said, "He did the right thing. Any means necessary to reach the end goal." Chelsea nodded her head in agreement.

"Well then, we should have led the fight with our strongest asset, and let Olivia use her Gift," Luca argued. I felt the color drain from my face. Something clicked in my brain, and I wasn't sure if it meant I figured out another piece of the puzzle or if I was becoming unhinged.

I was flooded with frustration. Luca kept secrets from me the whole time I knew him. Maybe I should have been more sympathetic considering recent circumstances, but it was just like Chelsea said it would be. Luca was the other Elste who had lived through the Gifted War. He felt terrible sorrow and reached rock bottom. Despite our friendship, he was desperate and willing to sacrifice my happiness. To him, I was a means to an end, and it made me angry.

Unlike Thisbe, I could foresee his plan, and I was as determined as ever not to let someone decide my fate for me. "So you are willing to throw me at the Meta without a plan, without a support system, without backing me up?" I asked, and the anger in my voice

94

was emphasized with the screeching of the car against the tracks as we went underground.

Luca took the bait. "No, I would never suggest throwing you to the wolves, but it's time you stepped up to the plate, Olivia. You are the strongest. You need to lead instead of standing in the shadows!" He was yelling by the time he spit out his last words.

"A careful leader comes up with a plan, rather than haphazardly jumping into the action!" I shouted.

"We have a plan. Find the Meta. Save our friends. You need to risk your own skin for once, and follow through!"

"And get myself killed? I'm surprised you even suggest it when less than twelve hours ago, you tried to kiss me!" His jaw dropped, and I wished I could take it back. I crossed the line in the heat of the moment.

"You did what?" Justin growled. His hands were balled into fists.

"I'm sorry, man. I had a few drinks," Luca apologized. It was too late. Justin's fist connected with Luca's face. Luca grunted with the influx of pain and fell back in his seat.

"Stop! We can't do this now! Stop!" I shouted. Justin lunged again, and they rolled to the floor. The other passengers looked up from their conversations. We were drawing too much attention to ourselves.

Luca covered his face, and Justin landed a punch into his gut. This was the opposite of rallying the troops. It wasn't what I meant to do.

"Olivia, stop them!" Carly bellowed. I had no choice. I clutched the charm that taunted me from around my neck. My Gift illuminated. I could smell my flowery scent. I bit my bottom lip and worked hard to isolate the sadness. I only wanted it to hit Justin and Luca, and as quickly as possible.

The train made a sudden sharp turn right. Luca and Justin were slammed into the wall. Blood dripped from Luca's nose. Justin wound up to swing again.

"Why isn't it working, Olivia?" Chelsea questioned me. I saw Justin's clenched jaw and the wrinkles on his forehead. He was fighting my Gift.

The train made another sharp turn, and Justin rolled off of Luca. They were both breathing heavily. Neon streetlights seeped through the windows as the train made its way aboveground again.

Justin stood up on his knees, still glaring at Luca, when one of the Asian women let out a terrified screech. The whole car turned to look, even Justin. The woman was visibly shaking. She pointed a judging finger at me and said, "You!" Then, she turned her phone around and there was a picture of me from the airport with the words DANGEROUS ELSTE plastered across my face.

The nerdy man next to us let out a haunted scream as the loading icon disappeared from his iPad and the same picture of me took its place. We must have regained cell service once we came aboveground.

"Look! Meta agents!" Lynn cried, nodding toward the car behind us. Pandemonium ensued. We had to get out of there fast.

* * * *

Chapter Twenty-Two: Rush of Danger

We hustled through the train cars, leaving havoc, colors, and scents in our wake. Each door we opened caused more panic among the passengers, and each door we closed couldn't keep out our pursuers.

Finally, the train stopped in the Bart station, and it couldn't have been soon enough. We had reached the last car. Chelsea and Lynn disappeared, but I could follow their trail as they pushed passengers out of the way and left the scent of vanilla and apples.

The automatic doors opened and we burst onto the platform. I gasped. What I saw was even more horrifying than on the train. The most technologically-savvy city in the world flashed my face everywhere. Warning signs were ubiquitous: as advertisements on the sides of buses, in the hands of every iPhone owner, on the storefronts of coffee shops.

Justin went into high security mode. "Come on," he ordered and grasped me by the elbow. The rest of our crew followed as we hiked up the cement hill in front of us.

"She's here!"

"That's her!"

"The female Elste!"

Morning joggers, finance professionals, and dog walkers pointed out their worst fears. It wasn't long before three Meta agents on bikes appeared at the bottom of the hill.

"This way," Justin commanded. We had reached a plateau halfway up. The streetlights glistened off an empty cable car's shiny maroon paint. He jumped on board and grabbed hold of the four-foot gearshift. It was wedged into the metal below.

I looked over my shoulder. The agents were swift on their bikes, closing in on the space between us. Out of breath, we all followed Justin onto the car without question. With one royal blue Gifted yank of the gearshift, the car tilted towards the edge of the plateau. There was a terrible screeching sound as the metal cables ground against each other.

"Hold on tight," Justin told us. My knuckles were white around the pole. I looked down the hill to see the agents fast approaching.

"Let's go!" Carly screamed. Her skin was unnaturally pale.

The car hit the tipping point, and the nose dipped down. There was no looking back. The wind picked up and whipped my hair behind me.

The Meta agents jammed on their brakes. The closest one reached out as the car passed them on the hill. Chelsea kicked him in the chest, and he tumbled backward.

Justin's teeth were clenched as he pulled on the only mechanism that kept the cable car from going out of control. The car fought back, letting out an awful noise that sounded like a dying whale. I was sure the whole city would wake up.

I looked behind us, and the three agents were back on their bikes. There was a slight turn around a grassy knoll. "We gotta get off!" I yelled. "Jump!" We all leaped and rolled.

"Keep moving," Lynn urged. I scurried to my feet and pushed forward, not sure which way was safe. A double-decker red tour bus rounded the corner.

"On here," Luca announced and sprinted to the open bus door. A lone driver was sitting sleepily in the driver's seat. He glanced at Luca through heavy lidded eyes. A puff of purple air burst around Luca. "Take us to the Golden Gate Bridge," Luca insisted, and we all piled on.

The agents rode their bikes across the grassy knoll, and were hot on our tail. "Get moving!" Luca commanded the driver. Under Luca's trance, he complied without saying a word.

I sat with my head turned to look out the window. The Meta agents were well trained. They managed to follow the bus, even as it ran red lights and cut through intersections.

I could see the orange red cables of the bridge glowing eerily from the moon's reflection off the fog. If we made it to the other side, I didn't know where we would go, but a bus out of the Meta-swarmed city was the best idea.

My heart vibrated in my chest as I sat. I felt so helpless. The surrounding hills closed in on the highway, and the claustrophobia made it hard to breath. It felt like it took hours when it was only minutes until we reached the bridge.

A tart smell filled our vehicle. I looked at Justin, quizzically. His face turned deep red like he was going to be sick. The bus spun out of control as the driver pulled the emergency break in the middle of the empty bridge.

"It's a mulberry elixir mist!" Justin said in horror.

"Get back here!" Luca shouted as the driver, no longer controlled by Luca's charm, sprinted out the door and away from the bus.

"Luca! You're not wearing your Gifted gear!" Lynn scolded. "Your Gift stopped working when we got on to the bridge."

Gusts of red tinted air was released from pipes on the side of the road. No wonder the bridge was empty. The Meta had setup the mulberry elixir to catch Gifted from escaping the city. We were sitting ducks.

"The Meta agents are still following us!" Chelsea announced. We all looked out the back window. "What do we do?"

The agents pedaled with fury. There was nowhere left to run. I grabbed Justin's hand. He returned my mournful gaze as if this was the end.

Suddenly, the ground started shaking. We were thrown around, violently, inside the bus.

"Earthquake!" Luca shouted. We were shaking like popping corn over a fire. I was scared beyond my wits. We were abandoned in the middle of a bridge that was almost one hundred years old. Large metal rivets fell from the suspended cables and echoed on the roof of the bus, like hail in a storm.

"The agents are retreating," Carly yelled in disbelief. Just as fast as it started, the rumbling came to a halt. I had survived a natural disaster, and there was nothing natural about it.

* * * *

Chapter Twenty-Three: Coit Tower

I leaned against the stone windowsill and stared into the Bay from the top of Coit Tower in San Francisco's North Beach. We had seen the famous landmark on Telegraph Hill and had made our way directly here without any other impediments. After the earthquake, the streets were abandoned. It was an odd and empty feeling, walking through the lonely city.

I must have had a grim look on my face because everyone had left me alone for most of the day. I told myself that I was thinking through a plan, but in truth, I was brooding.

Luca was right. What type of leader was I? I had let Graham get captured by the Meta. The room was so lit with Gifted colors and smells that I was surprised we didn't lead the Meta directly to us.

Justin came up behind me, wrapped his arms around my waist, and rested his chin against my head. I was happy Justin didn't bring up Luca's kiss. I felt warm and safe. I wanted to stand like that forever, but I couldn't. I let out a breath, emptying my lungs. Shying away from the trouble that lay ahead was impossible.

I turned around so Justin's arms locked behind me. "I know Graham made the decision to storm the Meta agents on his own, but I can't help feeling responsible. If I'm the most powerful Gifted in the world, how come I can't protect my friends?" I asked him.

"You will save everyone," he said.

"How can you be so sure?"

The corners of his lips turned up. "Because you care," he replied.

"And you don't?" I pressed.

His hands cupped my cheeks. He leaned in and brushed his lips against mine. My heart skipped a beat. He leaned back to look into my eyes and said, "The amount I care for you overshadows my feelings for everyone else."

I smiled, even though it wasn't true. "You care about others more than you let on," I told him. "You care about Marie." He closed his eyes, like it was a painful reminder.

"I can't believe my real grandmother is the Chancellor of the Meta, and Prometheus is my great-grandfather." Justin's voice was dreary.

"We'll make things right…for Marie…for Aunt Ev…and all the Gifted people the Chancellor has wronged," I promised Justin. He held me close, like he was clutching that thought.

I leaned my cheek against his chest and looked out the window again. An eerie, colorful mist surrounded Alcatraz Island. Bill was relieved when we finally made it to Coit Tower. He told us Alcatraz was where the Chancellor housed the Meta and kept its prisoners.

While we were holed up in our makeshift fort, he felt compelled to break the tension and share some stories. He worked for the state, protecting national monuments. He told us Native Americans kept away from the island that housed Alcatraz, believing it to be cursed. The old structure that covered its shore was bland except for the lighthouse and the rusty metal bars that covered every window. Yet somehow it made me shudder.

The strong smell of vanilla harassed my senses as Chelsea came next to me and looked out the window at the spooky island. "I would have never guessed that the Chancellor of the Meta was bunking with Al Capone and Machine Gun Kelly at Alcatraz," she announced. She had just come back from spying invisibly on Meta agents throughout San Francisco, and she was pumped up.

"There are Meta agents everywhere - marching up Lombard Street, lining up along Fisherman's Wharf, even plotting in the gardens at Golden Gate Park," Chelsea told us, her voice bright with excitement even as she paced the room.

She walked towards me again with her eyes wide. "And the agents weren't the only ones out and about. There were Gifted using their Gifts right in front of us - businessmen rushed by in colorful blurs to catch the Muni and bums smelled like garbage mixed with cinnamon sending sparks from their fingertips to light a fire. I even saw a woman disappear in a huckleberry *poof* when she passed an ex-boyfriend."

"And the Meta agents don't arrest them?" Carly asked.

"They would, but the Gifted are careful not to let the Meta agents see them," Chelsea replied.

The words flowed endlessly from her. "The agents are less discreet. Well, that's because they are dumb and don't realize we can overhear everything they say. One Meta agent was describing how the whole island of Alcatraz is protected by the mulberry elixir mist. Crazy!"

Lynn put her hand on Chelsea's shoulder to calm her. "We also heard them talking about the female Elste. The Chancellor is still spreading rumors about the havoc Olivia might create if she isn't controlled. Agents and Gifted alike are terrified," she explained. I let out a frustrated breath.

Lynn faced me and said, "They know you are in San Francisco. There are agents looking for you, and it's not just hearsay from panicked pedestrians. The agents were given orders to find you."

I nodded. They confirmed everything I already feared. "We're going out again," Lynn announced.

"You can't!" Carly yelled, throwing her arms in the air in frustration. "It's too dangerous."

Lynn raised her hands to stop her. "The agents were muttering about a Gifted uprising. If that's true, we need those Gifted on our side. We need to gather everyone we can."

"That's nuts! You'll end up arrested, just like Graham," Carly shouted.

"Graham did the honorable thing. He showed real valor by jumping into the fire pit," Chelsea spat.

Carly marched forward with her hands on her hips. The room smelled like a lush green meadow from her amplified Gift. Before the room exploded in flames from her fingers, Luca went to her and wrapped his arm around her shoulders. She turned her head to look at him. Her eyes were pleading for his help.

"Let's ask Olivia what to do, she's our leader," he said. I knew why he asked me to make the decision. After the fight on the train, he thought I would play it safe in order to protect the people around me. However, look where that landed us. We lost more friends each day. We needed to end the helpless act.

All eyes focused on me. The pressure to make a decision was mounting. "They should go. Like Lynn said, we need all the help we can get," I announced. Chelsea smiled broadly, Lynn nodded her head approvingly, and they were out the door without another word. Carly stamped her foot and pulled her arms across her chest.

"Is this the new order of command?" Luca asked, coolly. "Tell people to jump off a cliff because Justin whispers the order in your ear? What happened to saving the lives of our friends? It's time you made decisions for yourself, Olivia."

He had no idea how wrong he was, letting people jump off the cliff was my choice. I was the commander in chief. Making decisions was difficult and not everyone was going to agree with me.

"This decision was all mine." I kept my eyes level with his. He had lost faith in me.

I caught a glimpse of the anger on his face being replaced by sadness as he crossed with Carly to the other side of the room. He brushed her hair off her face. She gave him a crooked smile in return.

I wasn't sure if I was making all the right judgments, but I knew one of them was correct. Luca and I weren't meant to be together. The fight to win my heart was over. He had lost me.

It wasn't only because I loved Justin more. Luca and I were too similar. We were both Elstes looking to keep balance in the world. Carly's feisty attitude ensured Luca fought for things he believed in just as much as Justin's lone wolf style reminded me that sometimes it's necessary to be selfish.

"It really is an honor to meet you," Bill whispered, breaking the awkward silence. I looked at him, a shy man standing in the shadows of the room. He smiled warmly. "...a real female Elste. It's unbelievably exciting for me."

I shook my head and walked closer to him. "I'm nothing special—just another girl in high school who is scared she might create the next Gifted War."

"There are people out there who want change. They believe you can bring it. And I believe it, too," he told me. Luca and Carly joined us on the far side of the room. Something told me that Bill was about to impart his wisdom to us, and we settled down on the cold stone floor in front of him.

"My wife's grandmother was an amazing Gifted Ikos. She told elaborate stories over family dinners about the time she saved a family from a burning building and when she won a gold medal for speed skating in the Olympics. Her incredulous and whimsical tales caused my wife and me to fall in love with the Gifted, even if we didn't have a Gift ourselves.

"Before we settled in San Francisco and had our son, we traveled the world researching the Gifted. I met lots of brilliant people and heard magical stories." He looked past us to another time when he carried less baggage on his shoulders.

"Evelyn Forte was one of those people. She opened her doors to both Gifted and non-Gifted. We watched her transform a generation and cultivate a unique culture. It was a dream come true," he reminisced. For the first time in awhile, I wasn't angry hearing Aunt Ev's story. It was hard to deny she was a humanitarian and a valiant fighter.

"When my wife and I were ready to settle down, about twenty-five years ago, we landed in San Francisco. It was a city that thrived on the same Gifted culture. With the birth of our own Ikos son and my wife's grandmother's Gifted jewelry, we wanted him to have room to spread his wings," he said. For a minute, I could feel his excitement, imagining what it must have been like with a Gifted child. Then, the happiness disappeared from his eyes.

"We didn't know the Meta was going to choose this city as their new headquarters. The Chancellor wanted ultimate control and power so she moved to a densely populated Gifted community. She gets her thrills from others' suffering, even sinking low enough to display it on TV or post it on the internet. It makes me sick," he said and looked down at his hands. I exchanged a glance with Justin. Feeling emboldened instead of ill-fated by the fact that Prometheus had stolen the Elste necklace from the Meta and tricked me into accepting it was another first. I was happy he did it, because now I would get the chance to fight.

"Where is your son now?" Luca asked.

Bill took a deep breath and said, "We taught our son to be proud of who he is. He joined a small group of Gifted who stood up to her. He has been in the Meta prison for months." He held back tears as his voice cracked.

I leaned in and put my hand over his. At that moment, I realized Chelsea was right. This quest wasn't only about our friends. It was about a lost generation of Gifted who are suppressed by a terrible dictator.

"How do you suggest we get to Alcatraz?" I asked Bill. His head shot up. His eyes were hopeful for the first time since we met him.

* * * *

104

Chapter Twenty-Four: Whacked

A few hours later, Chelsea and Lynn still hadn't returned. There was no more time to waste. Bill secured us a fishing boat a friend lent him. We wanted to go before dawn. In fact, the more I thought about it, we needed to go. I was sick of playing defense. The longer we sat around, the sooner the Meta could sweep in and surround us. At least, what was left of us.

I stood tall on the end of the pier. My hair was a frizzy mess from the thick fog that hugged the ground. It clung to my cheeks and made it difficult to see in front of me, but I was resolved to press on. I lowered myself into the flimsy boat and tucked the cape Aunt Ev had given me around my arms.

I sat next to Justin. He grabbed hold of my hand, and I felt his Gift buzz through my blood. It gave me strength.

Luca and surly Carly sat across from us. Luca's face was determined. Carly was biting her nails, looking small as she hunched over. When she was quiet and timid like this, it was obvious she was younger than the rest of us. I tried to push the thought to the back of my mind. I couldn't afford to spend time worrying about her. I'd let Luca do that.

Bill waved good luck to us as Luca revved the teeny engine, and we bucked towards Alcatraz. The little boat cut through the water, and we were on our way to face the mighty Chancellor of the Meta, the same woman who captured hundreds of brave and intelligent Gifted who defied her. I should have had a better plan than tapping her on the shoulder and saying, "Release my friends, or else a sixteen year old Elste, your Gifted grandson, and their little buddies will get you!"

The four of us were silent as the boat moved through the bay. I wondered what the others were thinking, but I didn't want to sound scared. I was supposed to be their fearless leader, the most powerful Gifted in the world.

The mist and fog taunted and confused us. We could barely see the outline of the buildings downtown. The red cables of the Golden Gate Bridge poked through massive clouds. It felt like we would never find the Rock, but when I took a deep breath and smelled mulberries, I decided we must be getting close.

"I think I see the lighthouse," Luca shouted and pointed in front of us. We all followed his finger, and that was our mistake.

A swift and silent patrol boat had come up behind us. Within seconds, three Meta agents jumped onto our boat. Carly let out a high-pitched screech. My heart hammered in my chest.

They each held a silver gun. I reminded myself they were filled with mulberry juice instead of bullets, but I couldn't help the sick feeling in my stomach when it was pointed at Justin and me. The first agent was a round, middle-aged man. He grabbed hold of Luca's hands and forced them behind his back. Luca grunted as he fought against the man's grip.

The second one was lanky and barely eighteen. He reached down and put Carly in a headlock. Heavy sobs rattled her body. When he pointed the gun at her head, she looked petrified.

Justin and I sat still with our hands raised in surrender. We didn't want them to have a reason to hurt Luca and Carly.

The third agent leaned over and flicked Luca's Gifted necklace. Luca bared his teeth and tried to shake himself free. "Now what would a bunch of Gifted teenagers be doing on a boat circling a national landmark at this time of night?" the short and sleazy agent asked.

We knew the agents would be overconfident with the mulberry elixir in the air; however, it wasn't the elixir that was keeping us in check. Unfortunately for them, we were wearing our protective gear and were as powerful as ever.

Luca and Justin looked to me for the signal to overtake them, but I kept very still. I decided finding Alcatraz would be simpler if the agents thought we were under their control, and took us directly to the prisons.

"Hey boss, check out this one," the agent holding Carly said. He grasped Carly's hand and thrust her Gifted ring towards the other agent. "Do you think this is the female Elste?" His eyebrows raised on his head, becoming scared and concerned. I sucked in a breath as the agents leaned in to take a look.

Before we knew what was happening, the short agent whacked Carly on the side of the head. Her eyes bulged for a split second, and then she was unconscious in her seat. Luca jerked against the agent holding him down.

"Why did you do that?" the youngest agent said while still holding Carly in his arms.

"If she is the Elste, the mulberry elixir won't work on her. She would have overtaken us," he stated, matter-of-factly. "Now, let's take her to the Chancellor."

We coasted through the water for another few minutes. No one said a word as the Rock came into view, but the short agent kept sniffing, skeptically, like he wasn't sure they whacked the right girl. I tried hard to tame my Gift, but my nerves made it difficult.

Luca glared at me. I reminded myself that sacrifices were made in war. Plus, Carly was going to be okay. I would make sure of that.

When we finally reached the shore, it was deserted. At least it looked that way. A sheen of sweat covered my face. I was sure there were agents hidden in every corner.

The short agent jumped on-to the dock and took off running with Carly before we could stop him. He must have sensed something was up.

I turned to the other two agents and felt my Gift shoot out like a rocket. Their scream was blood curdling. I sent them into a never-ending depression, haunted by dark corners and black holes. It probably wasn't the best way to keep under the radar.

"Run!" I shouted at Luca and Justin as I stood my ground and unleashed my fury. They sped toward the main building.

The middle-aged agent grasped his skull between his hands, falling to his knees at the base of the boat. The teenager was down on all fours shaking his head viciously in hopes of reducing the pain. When I felt like the agents had suffered enough to keep them from running after me, I turned and followed Luca and Justin.

My cape and my hair blew back in the wind. The surge of power was intoxicating. I felt strong and brave as I stepped into the entrance of the creepiest prison in the world.

* * * *

Chapter Twenty-Five: A Single Spark to Light a Fire

"We need to go after Carly," Luca announced as we stood in the entrance panting.

I nodded in agreement, and said, "You save Carly. We'll find the rest of our friends."

Luca narrowed his eyes, surprised and angry that I agreed to split up. "I don't know what has gotten into you, but fine," he said with a clenched jaw.

I choked down the guilt from disappointing him. We had no choice. We were running out of time, couldn't he see that? I stuck out my chin in defiance as I watched him head in the same direction as the agent carrying Carly. I was going to stick to my way of doing things. I was the powerful female Elste, and I planned to act like it.

"Hey, Luca!" Justin shouted to get his attention. Luca paused and turned, without saying a word. "Look for a way to shut off the Meta's supply of the mulberry elixir."

Luca nodded once, like a soldier given orders from one of his commanders, but Justin wasn't done giving instructions. "Don't let the choices of a family that was forced upon you define who you are."

I was filled with pride as Justin echoed the words I had shared with him twenty-four hours ago. Whether it was Thisbe's selfish love or Luca's parents playing both sides for personal gain or the Chancellor's obsession with cleansing the world of Gifted people, we all had family who embarrassed us.

"We're your Gifted family," Justin ended. His words warmed my heart.

"Yes, sir," Luca replied, and his bright smile appeared, briefly.

"Where do we go now?" Justin asked me. I was happy someone had confidence in my leadership skills.

Something flashed bright gold behind Justin. I rushed to a vent on the floor. We stared at it for five seconds...twenty seconds...forty-five seconds. Nothing happened.

"Do you smell that?" I asked. I took a deep breath in and smelled lemons. It could have been the scent of the Meta's cleaning tools, but I highly doubted the stone walls had seen a sponge in decades.

Justin and I got down on our hands and knees. "It's Ms. Magos," Justin said. I nodded in agreement.

A spark shot through the grated metal, and we both jumped back. Ms. Magos was definitely below us. As quickly as possible, we got up and searched for stairs. We barreled down as fast as our legs would take us. As we reached the bottom step, Justin stuck out his arm to stop me. He brought his finger up to his lips to keep me quiet.

"Stop using your freaky powers," a husky male voice shouted from down the hall.

"Aww, big bad Meta agent is scared of a teenie weenie spark?" Max mocked.

Thud! "Doesn't hurt! Maybe you're not trying hard enough," Max said, pushing the agent's buttons.

Whack! Thud! "Nope, still don't feel it," Max insisted, even though his voice was strained.

"Max, stop!" Ms. Magos shouted.

"You want some of this, too, freak?" the agent taunted.

Smack! "Ow!" Ms. Magos wailed out in pain.

I pushed past Justin's arm and strode down the hallway. I could see the evil smirk of the Meta agent's profile. On the other side of the metal bars, he held a wood baton, ready to be used again.

Despite being hunched over to prepare for the pain, Ms. Magos held her ground in front of Max. The air around them flickered in a red glow, like Max could only turn on his Gift for a few seconds at a time despite his intense anger.

"Back off!" I shouted, about ten feet from them. The Meta agent turned his ugly sneer toward me. I threw my Gift with such force that you could see where it pierced the air.

My rage was uncontrollable and the smell of roses was suffocating, but the impact was even worse. The gloom I sent the Meta agent caused complete emotional darkness. I didn't give him a chance to fight. His eyes rolled to the back of his head as his knees gave out and he fell to the ground. I stepped over him without a second glance.

"Max," I whispered his name like I couldn't believe it was actually him. My body sagged with relief. He was proof that the rest of our friends were alive.

"Hot superhero getup, Liv. Did you steal it from Wonder Woman?" Max asked. I snorted at his joke, and it cleared my head. I had to be careful. My emotions heightened my Gift. I needed to concentrate and keep moving.

"It protects Gifted from the mulberry elixir. Not that a female Elste needs it, but I wanted to show where my loyalties lie," I said and looked back at Justin. He walked over, decked out in similar, but more masculine gear. "Speaking of Gifts, how did you manage to use yours? I can smell the mulberry elixir in the air, but we saw your sparks through the vent."

Max winked at me. "The Meta set up these cells to disable the Gifted, but they forgot about protecting themselves from Pandora High School's mischief mastermind. We've been stuffing the vents that release the elixir with the garbage they give us as food. In another day, we would have clogged the vent and overpowered the guard on duty. I guess you saved us the trouble." Max gave me a broad smile. I had to hand it to him. It was clever.

I took a good look at Max and his sister. They looked ragged and disheveled in grey prisoner gear, but it was so good to see them. I reached through the bars and pulled Max into a hug.

"Easy tiger, how about you let us out of the cell before you get too excited," Max said.

Justin approached the bars. "Stand back," he warned.

Placing both hands on the metal, he took a deep breath in and closed his eyes. When he released the breath through his nose, a deep blue hue surrounded his strained hands. His mouth was set in concentration.

I shifted my weight uncomfortably. It felt like we were in an airplane, flying straight up. The pressure that was sucked from the room and pulled toward Justin was unbelievable. Beneath his hands, a royal blue liquid dripped like spilled blue blood. The bars began to vibrate, and Justin let out a manly grunt.

His whole face turned red as he exerted the effort, and his body shook as much as the bars. It looked painful. I was about to stop him when the metal began to move. Justin let out a noise that only a man could make sound sexy, and the metal bent some more. Finally, he released the metal and stumbled backwards. The space was just wide enough for Max to step through.

"Thanks, man," Max said and patted Justin on the back like he helped him with a math problem instead of escape from prison.

Ms. Magos had been especially quiet since we showed up. She exited the cell and kept her eyes on the ground. I let her have her space. After all, she had been locked in a prison cell for weeks. I was about to suggest we get moving when she took a deep breath and set her wide, apologetic eyes on me.

Despite her tattered appearance, she looked more like my trusted global history teacher than she had in months. She took both of my hands in her own and said, "I know my words don't make up for my actions, but I'm sorry, Olivia. You are brave and loyal. I wish I could be more like you."

My cheeks flushed from the compliment. "Don't worry about it. Water under the bridge," I said, smiling at her. I was happy to have earned a loyal follower.

"Liv," Max said, looking worried for the first time. "How's Chelsea?"

"She's fine, Max," I said, and nodded my head vigorously. I wasn't sure if I was trying to convince him or myself. I didn't want to tell him that she was on a dangerous mission to gather Gifted in a city covered with Meta agents, and I hadn't seen her in hours.

I swallowed because my throat became dry all of a sudden. "How are Jamie, Derek, and Helen?"

He shrugged his shoulders. "I don't know. I haven't seen them since we got here."

I panicked. "We need to find them. Let's go," I commanded and started down the hall.

"What about Hunter?" Ms. Magos asked. She pointed in the cell. I gasped. Lying in the back, bloodied and bruised, was Hunter. He looked nothing like the strong, clever, and confident Horus that hung on Prometheus's every word. He was a fallen soldier, and I tried not to imagine the others looking the same.

"What happened to him?" I asked in astonishment.

"He tried to fight the Chancellor, but her Meta agents got to him first," Ms. Magos stated. I realized he was another friend I couldn't spend time worrying about.

"Get him help. We'll find Jaime, Derek, and Helen," I told them.

I watched Max swing Hunter's arm over his shoulder and help him to his feet. Through the rips in his shirt you could see blood dripping from gashes. The Chancellor had done a number on him. I hoped we didn't run into her before we found the rest of our friends.

* * * *

Chapter Twenty-Six: It's Just Politics

We heard a painful scream as Justin and I turned the corner. "Helen!" I said. My breath had caught. What were they doing to her? I prayed she wasn't with the Chancellor.

We took off running toward her voice. We passed through cold cellblocks and weaved through dank halls. My legs wouldn't move fast enough. I wished I had Graham's Gifted speed. Finally, the building no longer surrounded us. We were at the edge of the island.

My eyes scanned the horizon. Helen had to be here, but my heart stopped as I realized we were face to face with the almighty Chancellor of the Meta, flanked by half a dozen of her loyal guard.

She looked similar to the woman who acted as Justin's Grandma, but something about the way she stood with her back straight was off-putting. There was no warmth or sweetness like Marie.

"You are predictable, Olivia Hart," she said. In a sleek maroon pantsuit and fake smile, she stood proud and confident like a politician. We were the same height, but it felt like she was looking down on me.

"One little noise from your best friend, Helen O'Reilly, who got caught up in your Gifted web of drama, and you come running," she said with a snotty ring to her voice. She took a step to the side, revealing a thin and tired Helen on her knees with her hands bound behind her back. She was breathing heavily and tears streaked down her dirty face.

I took one step forward and the Chancellor blocked Helen again.

"Not so fast, Ms. Hart. We're not done here," she told me. The ground beneath us began to rise. The Chancellor, her Meta agents, Helen, Justin, and I were on a platform that jutted out of the bedrock. I bent my knees and put my arms out to steady myself.

The Chancellor took a dramatic breath in and said, "Do you smell that? It's the scent of another Meta victory. I turned off the elixir mist in your honor, Olivia Hart." She sent me another toothy grin. "Not that it works on you, but your pal, Jaime Forte, will need her Gift tonight." I didn't like the way she said my friend's full names. She knew too much about us.

The platform creaked and turned clockwise. Jaime's strained face came into view. Her arms were extended over the cliff. She was holding onto something with so much Gifted strength that I practically choked on her lavender scent.

"Jaime!" I shouted.

"Olivia! Don't come closer!" Derek screamed from somewhere over the edge. His voice was sharp.

"I'd listen to your big brother, Olivia," the Chancellor warned. "You see that Meta agent holding an elixir gun to Jaime's head? He's under strict orders to pull the trigger if you take another step toward her. And when Jaime gets soaked with the mulberry elixir, Derek goes bye-bye." She waved her hand.

I stood still, but my mind was racing. This was exactly what I feared for weeks when I promised not to put any of my friends in danger. Now it was too late. Who should I save first? Could I save any of them? Sweat dripped down my back.

"What do you want?" I said and balled my hands into fists.

The Chancellor raised her eyebrows. "Aww, sweet, innocent, Olivia. I don't want anything from you. In fact, I want you and my disgrace of a grandson to disappear," she said. It was the first time she stopped smiling, and also the first time she mentioned Justin.

"So you know?" Justin asked her. His voice was full of surprise and hurt. Marie said the Chancellor gave birth to Justin's mother and then disappeared from her life. We weren't sure if she knew about Justin at all.

"Know that my grandson has embarrassed me by becoming the one thing I loathe, Gifted? Yes," she said, dismissively. "I know all about your pitiful group of friends, Evelyn Forte's plot, and my sister's broken promises. I have eyes and ears everywhere. I am the most powerful person in the world and all without a disgusting Gift!" Her hands were gesturing wildly, and her mouth was twisted into an angry snarl.

Did she say she wasn't Gifted? Marie told us about the package she received from a distant Gifted relative.

The Chancellor took a deep breath. "You are going to help my campaign," she told us, smoothing her perfectly ironed power suit.

She pointed to the agent who held Helen. "Have her join Olivia's brother."

They lowered Helen over the edge to some sort of carrier we couldn't see, but by the look on Jaime's strained face, it was on the end of the rope she was holding. I could hear Helen whimpering, and it broke my heart. Justin reached for my hand and locked our fingers.

"Here's how this is going to work. You will use your horrible Gift on me. It will prove just how dangerous you are. Then, you will let my agents overtake you, proving my army's strength," she informed us. Video cameras rose out of the ground. "We will post it on every social media site -- YouTube, twitter, Facebook -- and show the world how the Meta protects its people."

"And if I don't cooperate?" I asked, swallowing a lump in my throat.

"Derek and Helen die," she said with a straight face.

I nodded my head like I understood and readied myself. I was stuck between a rock and a hard place. If I had to sacrifice my reputation for my friends, I was more than willing to do it.

This was it. This was the end. Or so I thought. There was an odd scuffling sound from the front of the building below. I peered over the edge and felt my face go pale. A heated mass of Gifted, dressed in ragged grey prisoner gear, were shouting and running to the threshold of the massive rock platform we stood on. Max, Ms. Magos, Graham, and even Hunter were at the head of the pack. They had managed to free all the Gifted prisoners.

I should have felt relieved, but I was panicked. I had already made my bargain with the Chancellor. My other friends didn't need to get involved.

The Chancellor took a step forward, but another buzz of noise grabbed everyone's attention. Boats landed on the other end of the island filled with more Gifted. They poured onto the land and marched toward us as well. Golden blonde hair was vivid in the sunlight. Chelsea and Lynn were leading the group.

The ground began to rumble again. The Gifted were fighting for their rights the best way they knew how, shaking the ground beneath the Meta and keeping the Chancellor on unbalanced footing. The unnatural earthquake made sense to me now. It was how the Gifted managed to get the agents off our tail when the bus stopped on the Golden Gate Bridge.

116

I looked back at the Chancellor, and was surprised to see she looked ecstatic instead of worried. "Prepare the elixir hoses," she commanded her Meta army and brought her clasped hands up to the sneer on her lips.

* * * *

Chapter Twenty-Seven: Brink of Death

Appearing indestructible, strong, and confident, the Chancellor marched forward with her arms open. "Hold back your anger, friends; I welcome you. Your timing is pristine. Tonight we will create history," she told the hundreds of Gifted that had just come rushing to the base of the platform like an angry mob.

There was utter silence. She began to pace along the front of the platform. "In moments, I will sacrifice myself to show you the Elste atrocities the Meta works hard to protect you from."

She had miraculously commanded their attention. They were shocked into listening to her politician speech. They didn't even notice her Meta agents aiming the nozzle of an elixir hose directly at them.

"Let me introduce you to the most selfish and dangerous female Elste the world has ever known," she said and stepped back to give the mob a better view of me. The group gasped. I shook my head to deny it. A low murmuring buzzed in the air. I could hear Max's voice in the crowd, shouting that it was lies. No one was listening to him.

"Her lack of a moral compass puts everyone at risk, Gifted and non-Gifted. Her relationship with this Horus is far worse than the original Pyramus and Thisbe. She blinds him from fairness and justice by pretending to love him," the Chancellor ranted. Justin's grip tightened on my hand. I could feel the hum of his Gift expanding with his anger. I didn't have to tell him that she was telling lies, but the mob of Gifted below didn't know me.

"Olivia, fight back!" Chelsea screamed. I bit my bottom lip. I was disappointing my friends. They didn't know she was blackmailing me. They couldn't see Jaime, Helen, and Derek dangling over the other side of the rock platform.

The Chancellor faced me, squared her shoulders, and said, "Do it! Try your best to defeat us. Isn't that what you came here to do? I just ask that you spare my friends." She fanned her hand to the crowd that waited with bated breath.

The seconds felt like hours. How could I protect everyone? If I exposed the Chancellor's plan, I would lose Jaime, Helen, and

Derek, and the Meta agents would cover the angry mob with the elixir anyway. Only the Chancellor would win.

There was a second option, though. If I went along with the Chancellor's plan and attacked her, she might spare Jaime, Helen, and Derek. I looked at Chelsea and already felt like I was disappointing her. The Meta agents were prepared with their elixir hose. They would never let the other Gifted escape.

It was a lose-lose situation, and I knew I had to make a tough decision. I thought of the unrelenting support Jaime, Derek, and Helen provided me, and how that same care brought them to the brink of death.

I swallowed hard and nodded. I would go along with the Chancellor's plan. If we were all put into prison cells, we might still have a chance to escape one day. I made a promise, and I was going to keep it. No one was going to die for me. I was the female Elste. I had a responsibility to fulfill.

I looked at Justin. Our hands were still locked together. His sad sea foam eyes reflected love and respect. He knew I had no other option.

My breathing was surprisingly calm even as my Gift grew and blossomed and flourished. The wind caught my hair and my cape, sending my rose scent backwards. I closed my eyes and let the power fill my body. It didn't overpower my senses like Thisbe. Perhaps I didn't feel the utter sadness that Thisbe felt when her best friend betrayed her, and when she lost her Pyramus. Instead, I was surrounded by love.

I was calm when I opened my eyes. I was ready to ruin my reputation to protect those I loved, but something grabbed my attention behind the Chancellor. With hundreds of eyes focused on me, I was the only one who noticed Luca and Carly on the side of the platform, turning a nozzle at the other end of the agent's hose to release the vat full of mulberry elixir into the bay!

I forced myself to keep a straight face, but inside I was ecstatic. There was another option. I could follow through with the Chancellor's plan, save Helen, Jaime, and Derek, and the Gifted people would be free from Meta control!

The only downside was that the Chancellor would succeed in proving that I am dangerous, and I would probably be locked up for life. The Gifted mob would help chain me up. I took a deep breath. It was a sacrifice I was willing to make.

I felt more confident than ever. I looked out from under my lashes and prepared my Gift when a frantic, macho scream cut through the silence from somewhere above us.

Everyone squinted and scanned the fog. Outstretched arms and legs made a beeline for the rock. Someone was skydiving and yelling at the top of his lungs.

Within seconds, Cliff Adams came into view with a parachute jutting out behind him. In perfect athletic form, he swooped in diagonally, scooped up Helen, and landed on the platform. He stood panting and holding her. He was absorbed in his concern for her safety and unaware of the battlefield he had dropped in on.

His rescue lightened the amount of weight that Jaime had to carry, and she managed to swing Derek onto the platform moments later. He took one step and shouted to the other Gifted, "the Chancellor was blackmailing Olivia!"

I braced myself for her wrath. She appeared eerily calm, like a great leader at wartime. She shouted, "THE ELIXIR HOSES, AGENTS!" The ground below turned into chaos as the mob tried to run away. The agents raised their nozzles and prepared to fire, but nothing came out. Luca and Carly had drained their reservoir. The agents panicked, dropped the hoses, and ran for cover.

"STAND GUARD! STAND GUARD!" the Chancellor bellowed, but the Gifted were already igniting their Gifts. For the first time, the Chancellor appeared worried, even shaken. She glanced at the video cameras that were feeding her social media empire as the drama unfolded.

She turned to run alongside her agents when Justin leaned over and shouted over the commotion, "She doesn't want anyone to know her darkest secret...that she is Gifted." He let go of my hand and opened both of his palms toward the Chancellor's back. A deep blue smoke billowed out. It mixed with the air and caused it to circle. Rain sliced the blue mass and pelted the ground.

The tornado blocked the Chancellor's escape route. She whipped around and sent Justin a piercing, fiendish look. Her polished hair was now flying wildly, and her ironed suit was soaked.

"How dare you insult my family and friends! It's time you apologized for the years of anguish you caused," Justin commanded.

His storm taunted her until she was at the platform's edge. She let out a frustrated screech, pulled a shiny Gifted knife out of her pocket, and threw her own storm at us.

It was tiny and unimpressive from lack of use, but it was all we needed to prove she was a liar. It stumbled toward us with barely enough speed to spin.

Justin blocked it, and I threw my hands out to attack her with my Elste power. Months of anger and frustration from feeling different and being lied to were released.

From the pit of my stomach, I built up my strength. I pictured Aunt Ev's mournful face left at the altar when her loved one was taken from her. I remembered Derek's broken heart when Lynn used him to get close to me. I felt the stab of pain caused by Helen's tears when she witnessed my Gift for the first time. Finally, I used the despair I felt when Justin said he couldn't love me anymore.

I blamed all these dreadful memories on the Chancellor and her hatred for the Gifted. It was with immense power and force that I attacked her and brought her to her knees, shaking in agony. I could feel the darkness leaving me and infecting her. I finally felt like I was living up to my name and protecting my friends and fellow Gifted.

It was therapeutic and remarkable. I felt strong and beautiful. I understood why it was so easy for Thisbe to lose control. I was intoxicating. Everybody, Gifted and non-Gifted, was silenced. They watched in awe as I overtook my enemy.

Then it was over, just as fast as it began. I dropped my arms, Justin's storms calmed, and we surrounded the bitter old woman.

Someone in the crowd behind us started chanting, "Elste, Elste, Elste."

* * * *

Chapter Twenty-Eight: Rehab

A sweet-smelling rainbow burst across the early morning sky as the Gifted celebrated their freedom from a tyrant who lay powerless on the floor. Derek wrapped me in a bear hug, and it felt unbelievable. I squeezed him back, relieved that he was alive and safe.

"Great job, V. I'm so proud of you," he gushed in my ear. Relief flooded me. It was finally over.

We looked out at the chanting crowd. "I think they found their new Chancellor," Derek told me.

I smiled and said, "Maybe we can ask Aunt Ev to do it. At least until I finish high school." He laughed and patted me on the back.

The rest of the Gifted Program was making their way to the top of the rock platform. I watched Derek's grin fade as Lynn came into his view.

"You have to speak to her eventually," I pointed out.

"I guess you're right. You're pretty smart for a kid sister," he observed, and then walked away.

Jaime, Chelsea, and Helen swarmed me with hugs, love, and congratulations, with Graham not far behind them. I was overwhelmed with happiness. I had managed to rescue all of them.

"I was about to climb the platform and knock some sense into you when the Chancellor told you to blast her with your Gift. I had no idea she was blackmailing you!" Chelsea exclaimed.

"We were lucky Cliff decided to drop in. I wasn't going to last much longer," Jaime explained.

"I was impressed," Graham told Jaime and flashed his flirty grin. Her cheeks turned a shade of red I had never seen before.

Graham wrapped his arm around her shoulder and said, "Hi, I'm Graham. A few months ago we wanted to kill each other. How's that for a first impression?" Jaime actually giggled, making my mouth drop open.

"Now I've seen everything," Chelsea joked and left the circle, Graham and Jaime following and chatting a few steps behind her.

Finally, it was just Helen and me. I grabbed both of her hands in my own, but before I could say a word, she said "Don't apologize for anything, Liv. You were great. I'm proud to be your best friend." She smiled.

A moment later, Cliff walked over, wrapped his arms around her, and breathed her in. I was happy for him. He got what he wanted without being Gifted. It was adorable until I noticed she was focused on someone else.

I followed her gaze, hoping Cliff wasn't doing the same thing. Her eyes were having an unspoken conversation with Derek! His crooked grin made me wonder what happened between them in the Meta's prison. I didn't have a chance to ask.

Hunter was making his way over with his arm wrapped around Prometheus. With all of Hunter's injuries, I wasn't sure who was supporting whom. It looked like nothing that happened in the past few weeks changed his loyalty to the old man. They stopped in front of the Chancellor and stood looking at her. Justin and I hurried over.

"I did what I had to in order to control my daughter," Prometheus said. He was unapologetic as he turned his gaze to Justin.

"Lies and manipulation. It's not the way I would have done it. I value people more than that," Justin said to his great-grandfather and wrapped his arm around me.

To our surprise, Prometheus gave him a genuine smile in return. "I'm proud of you," he said. It wasn't a happy family reunion, but I didn't expect much.

"What are you going to do with your daughter?" I asked, assuming he would take responsibility for her.

"I think it's time for a little rehab at Fort Bliss," he said. "Hunter, help me take our new guest home."

The last few weeks of the school year were a breeze, without any Gifted trouble. Plus, the new school superintendent, who replaced Mr. Dimon, excused us from Mr. Rowling's final paper and Mr. Stackhouse's lab assignment.

Things were going so smoothly that I never would have guessed what I was about to hear as I hopped into Justin's car to go with him for some lazy summer ice cream.

My phone buzzed in my lap, and I flipped it over to see AUNT EV flashing on the incoming call screen. "Hello, Chancellor," I sang as I put the phone to my ear.

"Olivia, we have a problem."

* * * *

About the Author

A year ago, Alana Siegel completed the level three Chartered Financial Analyst exam, and her fiancé accepted a job at Apple as an iPhone Developer. They decided it was an opportune time to move from New York to San Francisco and try something new. An engagement ring, a move 3,000 miles across the country, and one adorable kitten named Zeus later, the third book in the Olivia Hart and the Gifted Program series was conceived!

Alana Siegel was raised on Long Island, New York. She was the valedictorian of Plainedge High School and graduated with a B.A. and double major in Finance and Accounting from the Leonard N. Stern School of Business at New York University. Since early childhood she has loved to read fantasy books. Add a little romance and a happy ending and in her eyes you have a perfect afternoon of reading.

Connect with Me Online

Facebook: http://www.facebook.com/public/Olivia-Hart
Twitter: https://twitter.com/#!/AlanaSiegel
Website: http://www.oliviahartbooks.com/
Amazon Author: http://www.amazon.com/Alana-Siegel/e/B006O3NOAK
Olivia Hart and the Gifted Program Goodreads page:
http://www.goodreads.com/series/72755-olivia-hart-and-the-gifted-program
The Retreat book trailer (NEW!): http://youtu.be/9mxDa4Puh88
The Charm book trailer: http://youtu.be/q5-v27F7hPg
Tumblr: http://makeeverymisadventureanadventure.tumblr.com/
Independent Author Network:
http://www.independentauthornetwork.com/alana-siegel.html

* * * *

Acknowledgments

Thanks to my charming and talented editor, Carol Weber!
Carol Weber's website: http://www.carolscorrections.weebly.com

* * * *

Made in the USA
Lexington, KY
18 July 2013